This Is a Voice from Your Past

## ALSO BY MERRILL JOAN GERBER

NOVELS

*An Antique Man*
*Now Molly Knows*
*The Lady with the Moving Parts*
*King of the World*
*The Kingdom of Brooklyn*
*Glimmering Girls: A Novel of the Fifties*

SHORT STORIES

*Stop Here, My Friend*
*Honeymoon*
*Chattering Man*
*This Old Heart of Mine*
*Anna in Chains*
*Anna in the Afterlife*

MEMOIRS

*Old Mother, Little Cat: A Writer's Reflections on Her Kitten,
Her Aged Mother...and Life*
*Botticelli Blue Skies: An American in Florence*
*Gut Feelings: A Writer's Truths and Minute Inventions*

# This Is a Voice
# From Your Past

NEW AND SELECTED STORIES

## Merrill Joan Gerber

Ontario Review Press ✦ Princeton, NJ

Copyright © 2005 by Merrill Joan Gerber
All rights reserved
Printed in the U.S.A.

Ontario Review Press
9 Honey Brook Drive
Princeton, NJ 08540

Distributed by W. W. Norton & Co.
500 Fifth Avenue
New York, NY 10110

**Library of Congress Cataloging-in-Publication Data**

Gerber, Merrill Joan.
    This is a voice from your past : new and selected stories / Merrill Joan
Gerber. — 1st ed.
      p. cm.
    ISBN 0-86538-113-5 (cloth : alk. paper)
    1. California, Southern—Fiction. 2. Suburban life—Fiction. 3. Middle
class—Fiction. I. Title.

PS3557.E664T44  2005
813'.4—dc22

                                       2004046025
First Edition

These stories first appeared in the following publications: "This Is a Voice
from Your Past," in *The Chattahoochee Review*; "I Don't Believe This," in *The
Atlantic*; "Tell Me Your Secret," in *The Southwest Review*; "Night Stalker," in
*Shenadoah*; "The Cleopatra Birds," in *The American Voice*; "We Know That
Your Hearts Are Heavy" and "Latitude," in *The New Yorker*; "A Daughter of
My Own," in *Redbook*; "Approval" and "Honeymoon," in *The Sewanee
Review*; "See Bonnie & Clyde Death Car," in *Chattering Man*; "My Suicides,"
in a slightly different form, in *Salmagundi*; "Dogs Bark," in a shorter
version, in *Ontario Review*.

For my precious daughters
Susanna, Joanna and Becky

# CONTENTS

This Is a Voice from Your Past

# This Is a Voice From Your Past

E VERY WOMAN gets a call like this sooner or later. The phone rings, a man says: "This is a voice from your past." If you're in the mood and the caller doesn't find you in a room where other people are (particularly your husband), and if you have some time to spare, you might enjoy playing the game.

"Who is this?" I said, when my call came.

"Don't you recognize my voice?"

"Not exactly."

"Alvord's class? Florida? Your senior year?"

I paused. There had been a number of young men in my life in college, in Florida, in my senior year—and most of them were in Alvord's class.

This call—the first from Ricky—came just after I had given birth to my second daughter; I was living in California. When the phone rang I was in the kitchen cutting a hot dog into little greasy pieces for my two-year-old's lunch, and at the same time I felt my milk coming down, that sharp burning pain in both nipples, like an ooze of fire.

"Janet?" His voice was husky, or he was whispering. "This is a serious voice from your past. You know who I am. I think of you all the time. And I work at the phone company, I get free calls, so don't worry about this long-distance shit. I can talk to you all night if I want to."

"Tell me who you are," I said, just stalling for time, but suddenly I knew and was truly astounded. I had thought of Ricky often in the kind of reveries which we all engage in when we count the lives that never were meant to be for us.

"You must know. I know you know."

"Well, it must be you, Ricky, isn't it? But I don't have all night. I have two babies now, and I'm feeding them right this minute."

"Is your old man there?"

"No."

"Good, get the kids settled down and I'll hold on. And don't worry, I'm not going to complicate your life. I can't even get to you. I'm in Pennsylvania—and out of money."

"Hang on." I did some things I had to do for the children and then talked to him with my big girl eating in her high chair a foot away from the frayed green couch where I reclined on a pillow, letting the baby suck from my breast. Ricky told me then that he couldn't write a word anymore, it was killing him, he was drinking all the time, he had six kids, his wife was running around with someone else, and could I believe it, he, *he*, was working for the fucking phone company.

"I'm sorry," I said. "I'm really sorry, Ricky."

It occurred to me that anything else I said would sound trite, like: "We all have to make compromises," or "Maybe at some point we have to give up our dreams." The fact was, I hadn't given up mine but pursued it with a kind of dauntless energy. I didn't count the dream that he might have been my true love because I knew even then, all those years ago, that it was impossible. When he read his brilliant stories in class, he was married and living with his wife in a trailer on the outskirts of the campus. He'd already written his prize-winning story that had brought our writing class to its knees, the one that was chosen later for an O. Henry Award.

Alvord, our professor, a famous and esteemed novelist himself, had informed us in class, in front of Ricky, that the boy had been touched by the wand of the muse—he spoke of Ricky as if a halo gleamed over his head. He made it clear that none of us would ever reach the heights (and should not hope to) for which this golden boy was destined. "A talent like his," he told us, "is like a comet. It appears only once every hundred years or so."

I clung to my own modest talent and I was working on it; I couldn't envy Ricky his, based as it was in Catholic guilt to which I had no access (his stories were all about sin and redemption); what I envied during that hungry, virginal senior year of college was his wife, the woman he held in his arms each night, the one whose face was caressed by the gaze of his deep-seeing, supernaturally wise marble-blue eyes.

The day he called me in California as I sat nursing my baby girl, feeling the electric suck of her pulsing lips sizzle in a lightning rod strike from nipple to womb, I remembered an image of Ricky that rose up like an illumination—we were in the university library. Ricky had come in alone and had chosen to sit across from me at one of the long, mahogany tables where I was studying. He had his magic pencil in his long fingers and was bent over his lined notebook paper to create whatever piece of brilliant, remorse-filled prose he was writing. A long lock of his dirty-blond hair fell across his forehead, and his fingers scribbled, bent like crab pincers racing over the lined notebook page, wrote words that according to Alvord would turn out to be second only to James Joyce's.

Ricky had told me that his wife worked in some office, typing business documents. He explained, in his breathy East Coast accent, that she was ordinary and dull and he had too young been seduced by her beauty, her astonishing breasts, and his own fierce desire. He assured me I knew him in a way that she never could. We had long earnest discussions after Alvord's class, and in the cafeteria over coffee, and on benches in front of the library—debates about literature and genius (who knows now if their content held anything more remarkable than youth and idealism cooked up in a predictable collegiate stew?).

Still, that night in the library, he stopped his work to stare intensely at me across the table time after time—but didn't smile. We were like conspirators, we knew we shared a plan, an ingenious plot to outfox time, mortality, death—we were both going to be famous writers, and we would—by our words alone—live forever.

At some point that evening—in his frenzy of writing—Ricky's cramped fingers relaxed, his head dropped sideways onto his arm on the tabletop, and he fell asleep in the library. He remained there, vulnerable and naked in my gaze, breathing as I knew he must breathe as he slept beside his wife in that trailer, his mouth slightly open, his blue-veined eyelids closed over his blue eyes, his nostrils flaring slightly with each breath.

I watched him till the library closed, watched his face and memorized every line of his fair cheek, the angle of his chin, watched fascinated as a thin thread of drool spooled from his slightly parted lips to the tabletop. I looked around me to be sure no one was near or watching. Then, before he woke, I very slowly moved my hand across the table and anointed the tip of my pencil with his silver spit.

The second time Ricky called me my husband *was* in the room. It was thirty years later, a day in late August. I—with a slow but certain fortitude—had written and published a number of novels by then. My three daughters were grown. The baby who had been at my breast at the time of his first call was in graduate school, and older than I had been when Ricky slept opposite my gaze in the library.

"Janet? This is a voice from your past."

A warning bell rang in my chest. At that moment I was busy talking to my husband about some family troubles (my mother had had a stroke and we were about to put her in a nursing home) and I felt rudely interrupted. I wasn't ready to engage in the game he wanted to play."

"Which past?" I said. "I have many."

"It's Ricky, your old buddy."

"Ricky! How are you?" I said his name with some enthusiasm because he expected it, but I felt my heart sink because I knew I would have to listen to his troubles and I had no patience just then. The game of "remember what we meant to each other" had lost its appeal since by this time everyone I loved filled up my life completely. I had not even a small chink of space left for a latecomer. "Are you still living in Pennsylvania?"

"No, I'm right here!"

"Right here?" I looked down into my lap as if I might find him there.

"In sunny California. In your very city. And I'm here for good."

"How did you know where to reach me? My number isn't even listed!"

"I found one of your books back east and on the cover it said what city you lived in. So when I got here—and I want you to know I picked this city to settle in because of *you*—I went to the library and asked the librarian. I knew a librarian was bound to know where the city's most famous writer lived. I told her I was your old buddy and she gave me your phone number."

"I'm not famous, Ricky."

"Me neither," he said. "How about that?"

I told him I would call him back in a half hour—and in that time I explained to my husband, more or less, who he was. An old college friend. A used-to-be-writer. A drunk. I don't know why I dismissed Ricky so unfairly. Something in his voice had put me on guard. And I could see that this tag with time was a game there was no sense in playing. I had settled into my ordained life like concrete setting in a mold, and I no longer trifled with the idea that I might want to change it. At least not by trailing after romantic visions. With a sense of duty, though, I phoned him back...and braced myself.

"You won't believe the stuff that's happened to me," he said. He laughed—he almost cackled—and I shivered. "Can we get together?"

When I hesitated, he said, "I've been through AA, I'm a new person. I'm going to join up here, too, of course. The pity is that before I turned myself around I lost every friend I ever had."

"How come?"

"How come? Because an alcoholic will steal from his best friend if he has to, he'll lie with an innocent face like a newborn baby. There's nothing I haven't stooped to, Janet. I've been to the bottom, that's where you have to be before you can come back. I've rented a little room in town here, and I'm hoping...well, I'm hoping that we can be friends again."

"Well, why not," I said. I had the sense my house had become a tunnel and I was getting lost in the dark.

"But mainly—I'm hoping you'll let me come to your class. I want to get started writing again."

"How did you know I teach a class?"

"It says on your book, Janet. That you teach writing at some university or other."

"Well, you certainly are a detective, aren't you?"

"I'm sly as a fox."

"I guess you could visit my class when it begins again after Labor Day. I'll tell my students that you studied with me in Alvord's class. Since most of my old students will be coming back to take the advanced class, they already know about Alvord. In fact, I quote him all the time. We use all his old terms—'action proper,' 'enveloping action'—his dedication to point of view. Maybe we can even get a copy of your old prize story and discuss it."

"Great. So when can we get this friendship on the road again?"

"Look—I'm having a Labor Day barbecue for my family and some friends on Sunday—why don't you come? Do you have a car?"

"I can borrow one."

"Do you need directions? I'll have my husband give them to you."

I called Danny to the phone and handed him the receiver. "Tell my friend Ricky the best way to get here." I wanted Ricky to hear Danny's voice, to know unequivocally that I was taken, connected, committed...that I wasn't under any circumstances available.

A stranger rang the doorbell, a man eighty years old, skin jaundiced, skeletal bones shaping his face. The golden hair was thin and gray. Only his voice, with an accent on his tongue like the young Frank Sinatra, convinced me he was the same Ricky. When I shook his hand, I felt his skin to be leathery, dry. When I looked down, the nails were bitten to the quick.

He came inside. I felt him take in the living room in one practiced glance—the art work, the decorations, the furniture—and then we passed out the screen door to the backyard where the party was in progress.

Danny was on the patio, grilling hamburgers and hot dogs over the coals. My three daughters, one already married, and two home from their respective graduate schools, looked beautiful in their summer blouses and white shorts. I saw the backyard as Ricky must have seen it—alive with summer beauty, the plum tree heavy with purple fruit, the jasmine in bloom, the huge cactus plants in Mexican painted bowls growing new little shoots, fierce with baby spines.

My other guests included my sister and her sons, my eldest daughter's husband, a few of my students, several women I had been in a book club with for the last fifteen years. Ricky looked around; I could feel him adding up my life and registering it in his bloodshot eyes.

I took him over to meet Danny and then said: "Let's go sit on the swings and talk." We tramped across the brilliant green of the grass to the old swingset where my daughters used to play. Ricky was wearing a formal gray wool suit, his bony frame almost lost inside its wide shoulders. He swung slowly back and forth, sitting on the splintery wood seat, his hands clutching the rusty chains. He talked looking forward, into air.

"My son Bobby is the one who invited me out to California. He made it big-time," Ricky said, and laughed.

"Is he in movies?" I asked.

"Not exactly. He dove into a city pool in Philly and broke his spine. Now he's in a wheelchair for life. I got him a sharp lawyer who brought a deep-pockets lawsuit against the city. Bobby was awarded a million and a half bucks, enough to take care of him the rest of his life and, if I play it right, take care of me, too! My other kids don't talk to me, so Bobby is my only salvation."

"But why is he in California?"

"He's living in a fantastic halfway house out here—the best in the world for paraplegics; Bobby gets all kinds of services, I even can bring my laundry over there and he'll get it done for me free. And he's got enough extra pocket money to help me pay my rent for a while till I get a job."

"What a terrible thing to happen to him."

"No, just the opposite. He was a beach bum, a loser. Now he's got it all together, the whole future taken care of. I think he's relieved. He can use his arms—he plays wheelchair basketball. He lifts weights. He gets counseling, he gets his meals served. Sometimes I wish I could change places with him. But no, I'm back at square one, looking for a job again."

"No more phone company?"

Ricky made a strangling noise in his throat. "I'm going to write my novel, Janet. Finally. I'm going to get it together before I die. If I can sit in on your class, I figure it will start my motor again. You probably teach something like the way Alvord taught us. That old magic. Maybe I can feel that excitement again. I'm counting on it, it's my last hope."

"Do you ever hear from Alvord? Did you stay in touch?"

"In touch! I *lived* with him for a year in Florida when I was really down and out. He took me in, told me he loved me like a son. The trouble was he didn't feed me, Janet. He offered me a place to stay on this farm of his, and then all I could find to eat in the house was Campbell's soup. I think one day he actually hid the bacon from me so I couldn't get my hands on it. So I had to take his truck into town with some money of his to get some food, but I'd been drinking again and I totaled it. He told me I had to leave. He gave me fifty bucks and bought me a train ticket back to Philly. But he was a pain, anyway, preaching to me all the time about being a man, taking responsibility for my kids. I swear, the man was a genius but he's losing it, Janet. He's in his eighties now. He used to think I walked on water."

"We all did."

"That's why I came to live near you. You're the only one on earth who really knows my genius."

I didn't actually count, but I had the sense Ricky ate at least five hamburgers, and as many hot dogs. He hung around the food table, his mouth going, not talking to anyone, but looking at my women friends, their faces, their forms. He looked my daughters up and down—there was no way to stop him. At one point he came to me and said, "Your daughters are really beautiful. All three of them. They have your soul in their eyes." I wanted to distract him. I asked him how often he saw his son; he said, "As often as I can, he gives me CARE packages. I don't have much food in the new place."

After our guests left, I packed up all the leftovers for Ricky: potato chips, lukewarm baked beans, the remaining coleslaw, a package of raw hot dogs and buns to go with them, a quarter of a watermelon, lettuce and sliced tomatoes, even pickles, even mustard and ketchup.

"Listen, thanks," he said. "You're a lifesaver. You don't know how lucky I feel to have found you again. Could I ask you one more favor, though? Would you mind if I came back tomorrow and used your typewriter? I need to write a letter to apply for a job. Someone gave me a tip about a job being night watchman in a truck yard. All I would have to do is sit in a little shed and watch for thieves. I figure I could write all night if I get it."

My reaction was instinctive; I knew I didn't want him back in my house again. "Why don't you let me lend you my electric typewriter? I use a computer now, so I won't need it for a while. I do love it, though—it's the typewriter I wrote my first novel on."

"Then maybe it will be lucky for me. I'll guard it with my life."

"Okay, give me a minute, I'll go put it in its case." I left him standing in the living room with my husband, but I heard no conversation at all—not even ordinary chatter. I could see why Danny was unable to think of a single thing to say to him.

Ricky finally left, laden like an immigrant—bags of food, paper, carbon paper, envelopes, stamps, my typewriter. He stuffed it all into the trunk of an old red car.

Danny and I watched him drive away. He didn't wave—he tore from the curb like one possessed.

"Funny guy," Danny said.

"I don't think we know the half of it," I told him.

I found Ricky's O. Henry prize story in a book and had thirty photocopies made for my students. At the start of class I distributed the copies and told my students that at 7:30 a guest was arriving, a writer of unique skill and vision, a man we were honored to have visit our class. I warned them about the pitfalls of the writer's life, how one could not count on it to earn a living, how so many talented writers fell by the wayside due to pressures of ordinary life. This visitor, I said, a very close friend of mine from the past who had missed what you might call "his window of opportunity," hoped to join our class and work as hard as anyone in it. "He had a whole life in between of doing something else he had to do. All of you are young, at the start of your first life, and if you really want this, this is the time to do it."

When Ricky arrived at my classroom, it was already almost nine PM. He apologized, saying the bus had been late. He was wearing a red V-necked sweater, and looked less cadaverous than at the barbecue, but still much older than his years. He seemed elated to find that a copy of his story was on every desk, and when one of the students asked him how he got the idea for it, he said, simply, "I had thought many times of murdering my brother."

By then, we were already in the midst of having another student read his story; I told the class that next week we would discuss Ricky's story.

I nodded for Harold to go on reading; his story was about a day in the cotton fields of Arkansas, and how the men, women and children picking cotton on a burning hot day reacted when the truck that delivered them failed to leave off drinking water. When the last line had been read, Ricky spoke out in the exact tones of our teacher, Alvord.

"It comes alive on the last page, finally, you see, because it uses all the senses. Since a crying baby can seduce a reader from the very death of Hamlet himself, the writer must bring everything to life. And you do, young man! You do!"

The class was silent, and then a few students applauded Harold and then everyone did—till his embarrassed smile lit up the room. I announced that we would take our usual ten-minute break. When the class had filed out, I thought I would find Ricky waiting to talk to me about my students, to tell me how the class had seemed to him, if it would suit his purposes. But he left the room without a glance in my direction, and when I looked out into the hall, I saw him in deep conversation with

one of my students, a young woman. When the class recon-
vened, neither one of them returned for the second half.

At seven the next morning, my student phoned me. "This is
Alice Miller. I'm so sorry to disturb you," she said, "but your
friend, the famous writer, borrowed my car last night. We
went out for coffee and afterward he said he had an urgent
errand to go on, he practically got on his knees to beg to
borrow the car. He said that although he knew I didn't know
him very well, *you* could vouch for him, and he promised he
would have my car back in my carport by midnight. He
borrowed ten dollars, too. He never came back. And I can't get
to work without it!"

"I'll see if I can reach him at the number I have for him," I
told her. "I'm so sorry. I'll call you right back."

But his landlady did not find him in his room. I called Alice
back and told her I could only imagine that there was some
emergency with his son who was a paraplegic. I reassured her
that he would surely have the car back to her very shortly but
in the meantime to take a taxi to work, that I would pay for it.

I learned later that when finally Ricky did return the car to
Alice, he never even rang her bell. He left the car at the curb.
She found the inside of it littered with cigarette butts, racing
forms, empty paper cups, and the greasy wrappers from
McDonald's hamburgers. The gas tank was totally empty.
There was not even enough gas left in the tank for Alice to get
to a gas station to fill it up.

Toward the end of September, I was about to apply for a
fellowship and realized that I needed my typewriter to fill out
the application form. My anger overcame my revulsion, and
I dialed the number Ricky had originally given me. His

landlady answered and informed me that he'd moved out bag and baggage—that "he shipped out to sea."

"To sea!" I imagined him on a whaling ship, thinking he was Melville, or more likely that he was one of the sailors in Stephen Crane's story about men doomed at sea, "The Open Boat," a piece of work whose first line Alvord had often quoted: "None of them knew the color of the sky."

But my typewriter! I wanted it, it was mine. I felt as if Ricky had kidnapped one of my children.

"Let it go," my husband said. "It's an old typewriter, I'll get you a new one, it doesn't matter. Write it off as a business loss. Write him off—your old friend—if you can as one of those mistakes we all make in life."

In the days following, I had trouble sleeping. I held imaginary conversations with Ricky, by turns furious, accusatory, damning, murderous. "I trusted you!" I cried out, and in return I heard his laugh...his cackle. Alvord had often talked about evil in his class: the reality of it, how it existed, how it was as real as the spinning globe to which we clung.

Days later, in a frenzy, I began calling hospitals, halfway houses, rehab clinics, trying to find the place where Ricky's son lived—if indeed he had a son.

"Don't do this to yourself," Danny said. He saw me on the phone, sweating, asking questions, shaking with anger, trembling with outrage.

But one day I actually located the boy. He was in a hospital in a city only a half hour's drive from my house. I named his name, Bobby, with Ricky's last name, and someone asked me to wait, she would call him to the phone. And a man picked up the phone and said "Yes? This is Bobby."

I told him I was a friend of his father, that his father had my typewriter.

"Oh sure, I know about that. You're his old friend. He left the typewriter here with me. You can come and get it." His voice had the same tones as Ricky's voice. The same seductive sound—the "Oh sure" a kind of promise, the "come and get it" the serpent's invitation.

"His landlady said he went to sea...?" I felt I must have another piece of the puzzle, at least one more piece.

"Yeah—he got a job teaching English on a Navy ship. I told him he better take it, he wasn't going to freeload off me the rest of his life."

"I'm sorry," I said to the boy. "I'm sorry about your accident...and about your troubles with your father."

"Hey, don't worry about it. It's nothing new. But if you want his address on the ship I could give it to you."

"No—thank you," I said. "I don't want it. I think your father and I have come to a parting of the ways. Good-bye, Bobby, I wish you good luck."

"You, too," Bobby said. "Anyone who knows my father needs it."

Then, two years after I talked to his son, I got the third phone call. "This is a voice out of your fucking past."

"Hello, Ricky." My heart was banging so hard I had to sit down.

"I heard from my son you want your goddamned type-writer back."

"No, no—"

"You'll have it back. It's in little pieces. I'll be on your doorstep with it in twenty minutes."

"I don't want it, Ricky. *Don't come here!* Keep it."

"I said you'll have it back. I *always* keep my word, you fucking..."

"Please, keep it. I don't need it! Keep it and write your book on it!"

"Just expect me," Ricky said. "I'll be there, you can count on it. Watch out your window for me."

And so I did. For a week. For a month. I keep watching and sometimes, when the phone rings, I let it ring and don't answer it.

# I Don't Believe This

A FTER IT WAS ALL OVER, one final detail emerged, so bizarre that my sister laughed crazily, holding both hands over her ears as she read the long article in the newspaper. I had brought it across the street to show it to her; now that she was my neighbor, I came to see her and the boys several times a day. The article said that the crematorium to which her husband's body had been entrusted for cremation had been burning six bodies at a time and dumping most of the bone and ash into plastic garbage bags which went directly into their dumpsters. A disgruntled employee had tattled.

"Can you imagine?" Carol said, laughing. "Even that! Oh, his poor mother! His poor *father!*" She began to cry. "I don't believe this," she said. That was what she had said on the day of the cremation when she sat in my backyard in a beach chair at the far end of the garden, holding on to a washcloth. I think she was prepared to cry so hard that an ordinary handkerchief would not do. But she remained dry-eyed. When I came outside after a while, she said, "I think of his beautiful face burning, of his eyes burning. " She looked up at the blank blue sky and said, "I just don't believe this. I try to think of what he was feeling when he gulped in that stinking gas. What could he have been thinking? I know he was blaming me."

She rattled the newspaper. A dumpster! Oh, Bard would have loved that. Even at the end, he couldn't get it right. Nothing ever went right for him, did it? And all along I've been thinking that I won't ever be able to swim in the ocean again because his ashes are floating in it! Can you believe it? How that woman at the mortuary promised they would play Pachelbel's Canon on the little boat, and the remains would be scattered with "dignity and taste"! His *mother* even came all the way down with that jar of his father's ashes that she had saved for thirty years, so father and son could be mixed together for all eternity. Plastic garbage baggies! You know," she said, looking at me, "life is just a joke, a bad joke, isn't it?"

Bard had not believed me when I'd told him that my sister was in a shelter for battered women. Afraid of *him*? Running away from *him*? The world was full of dangers from which only *he* could protect her! He had accused me of hiding her in my house. "Would I be so foolish?" I had said. "She knows it's the first place you'd look."

"You better put me in touch with her," he had said menacingly. "You both know I can't handle this for long."

It had gone on for weeks. On the last day he called me three times, demanding to be put in touch with her. "Do you understand me?" he threatened me. "If she doesn't call here in ten minutes, I'm checking out. Do you believe me?"

"I believe you," I said. "But you know she can't call you. She can't be reached in the shelter. They don't want the women there to be manipulated by their men. They want them to have space and time to think."

"*Manipulated*?" He was incredulous. "I'm checking *out*, this is *it*! Goodbye forever!"

He hung up. It wasn't true that Carol couldn't be reached. I had the number. I had not only been calling her, but I had also been playing tapes for her of his conversations over the phone during the past weeks. This one I hadn't taped. The tape recorder was in a different room.

"Should I call her and tell her?" I asked my husband.

"Why bother?" he said. He and the children were eating dinner; he was becoming annoyed by this continual disruption in our lives. "He calls every day and says he's killing himself and he never does. Why should this call be any different?"

Then the phone rang. It was my sister. She had a fever and bronchitis. I could barely recognize her voice.

"Could you bring me some cough syrup with codeine tomorrow?" she asked.

"Is your cough very bad?"

"No, it's not too bad, but maybe the codeine will help me get to sleep. I can't sleep here at all. I just can't sleep."

"He just called."

"Really," she said. "What a surprise!" But the sarcasm didn't hide her fear. "What this time?"

"He's going to kill himself in ten minutes unless you call him."

"So what else is new?" She made a funny sound. I was frightened of her these days. I couldn't read her thoughts. I didn't know if the sound was a cough or a sob.

"Do you want to call him?" I was afraid to be responsible. "I know you're not supposed to."

"I don't know," she said. "I'm breaking all the rules anyway."

The rules were very strict. No contact with the batterer, no news of him, no worrying about him. Forget him. Only female relatives could call, and they were not to relay any news of him—not how sorry he was, not how desperate he was, not how he had promised to reform and never do it again, not how he was going to kill himself if she didn't come home. Once I had called the shelter for advice, saying that I thought he was serious this time, that he was going to do it. The counselor there—a deep-voiced woman named Katherine—said to me, very calmly, "It might just be the best thing; it might be a blessing in disguise."

My sister blew her nose. "I'll call him," she said. "I'll tell him I'm sick and to leave you alone and to leave me alone."

I hung up and sat down to try to eat my dinner. My children's faces were full of fear. I could not possibly reassure them about any of this. Then the phone rang again. It was my sister.

"Oh God," she said. "I called him. I told him to stop bothering you, and he said, 'I have to ask you one thing, just one thing. I have to know this. Do you love me?' My sister gasped for breath. "I shouted *No*—what else could I say? That's how I *felt*, I'm so sick, this is such a nightmare, and then he just hung up. A minute later I tried to call him back to tell him that I didn't mean it, that I did love him, that I do, but he was *gone*." She began to cry. "He was gone."

"There's nothing you can do," I said. My teeth were chattering as I spoke. "He's done this before. He'll call me tomorrow morning full of remorse for worrying you."

"I can hardly breathe," she said. "I have a high fever and the boys are going mad cooped up here." She paused to blow her nose. "I don't believe any of this. I really don't."

Afterward she moved right across the street from me. At first she rented the little house, but then it was put up for sale and my mother and aunt found enough money to make a down payment so she could be near me and I could take care of her till she got her strength back. I could see her bedroom window from my bedroom window—we were that close. I often thought of her trying to sleep in that house, alone there with her sons and the new, big watchdog. She told me that the dog barked at every tiny sound and frightened her when there was nothing to be frightened of. She was sorry she had gotten him. I could hear his barking from my house, at strange hours, often in the middle of the night.

I remembered when she and I had shared a bedroom as children. We giggled every night in our beds and made our father furious. He would come in and threaten to smack us. How could he sleep, how could he go to work in the morning, if we were going to giggle all night? That made us laugh even harder. Each time he went back to his room, we would throw the quilts over our heads and laugh till we nearly suffocated. One night our father came to quiet us four times. I remember the angry hunch of his back as he walked, barefooted, back to his bedroom. When he returned the last time, stomping like a giant, he smacked us, each once, very hard, on our upper thighs. That made us quiet. We were stunned. When he was gone, Carol turned on the light and pulled down her pajama bottoms to show me the marks of his violence. I showed her mine. Each of us had our father's handprint, five red fingers, on the white skin of her thigh. She had crept into my bed, where we clung to each other till the burning, stinging shock subsided and we could sleep.

Carol's sons, living on our quiet adult street, complained to her that they missed the shelter. They rarely asked about their father and occasionally said they wished they could see their old friends and their old school. For a few weeks they had gone to a school near the shelter; all the children had to go to school. But one day Bard had called me and told me he was trying to find the children. He said he wanted to take them out to lunch. He knew they had to be at some school. He was going to go to every school in the district and look in every classroom, ask everyone he saw if any of the children there looked like his children. He would find them. "You can't keep them from me," he said, his voice breaking. "They belong to me. They love me."

Carol had taken them out of school at once. An art therapist at the shelter had held a workshop with the children every day. He was a gentle, soft-spoken man named Ned, who had the children draw domestic scenes and was never once surprised at the knives, bloody wounds, or broken windows that they drew. He gave each of them a special present, a necklace with a silver running-shoe charm, which only children at the shelter were entitled to wear. It made them special, he said. It made them part of a club to which no one else could belong.

While the children played with crayons, their mothers were indoctrinated by women who had survived, who taught the arts of survival. The essential rule was: *Forget him, he's on his own, the only person you have to worry about is yourself.* A woman who was in the shelter at the same time Carol was had had her throat slashed. Her husband had cut her vocal cords. She could only speak in a grating whisper. Her husband had done it in the bathroom with her son watching. Yet each night she sneaked out and called her husband from a nearby shopping center. She was discovered and disciplined by the administration; they threatened to put her out of the shelter if she called him again. Each woman was allowed space at

22

the shelter for a month while she got legal help and made new living arrangements. Hard cases were allowed to stay a little longer. She said she was sorry, but he was the sweetest man, and when he loved her up, it was the only time she knew heaven.

Carol felt humiliated. Once each week the women lined up and were given their food: three very small whole frozen chickens, a package of pork hot dogs, some plain-wrap cans of baked beans, eggs, milk, margarine, white bread. The children were happy with the food. Carol's sons played in the courtyard with the other children. Carol had difficulty relating to the other mothers. One had ten children. Two had black eyes. Several were pregnant. She began to have doubts that what Bard had done had been violent enough to cause her to run away. Did mental violence or violence done to furniture really count as battering? She wondered if she had been too hard on her husband. She wondered if she hadn't been wrong to come here. All he had done—he said so himself, on the taped conversations, dozens of times—was to break a lousy hundred-dollar table. He had broken it before; he had fixed it before. Why was this time different from any of the others? She had pushed all his buttons, that's all, and he had gotten mad, and he had pulled the table away from the wall and smashed off its legs and thrown the whole thing outside into the yard. Then he had put his head through the wall, using the top of his head as a battering ram. He had knocked open a hole to the other side. Then he had bitten his youngest son on the scalp. What was so terrible about that? It was just a momentary thing. He didn't mean anything by it. When his son had begun to cry in fear and pain, hadn't he picked up the child and told him it was nothing? If she would just come home he would never get angry again. They'd have their sweet life. They'd go to a picnic, a movie, the beach. They'd have it better than ever before. He had just started going to a new church that was helping him to become a kinder and more sensitive man. He was a better person than he had ever been; he now knew the true meaning of love. Wouldn't she come back?

One day Bard called me and said, "Hey, the cops are here. You didn't send them, did you?"

"*Me*?" I said. I turned on the tape recorder. "What did you do?"

"Nothing. I busted up some public property. Can you come down and bail me out?"

"How can I?" I said. "My children…"

"How can you *not*?"

I hung up and called Carol at the shelter. I told her, "I think he's being arrested."

"Pick me up," she said, "and take me to the house. I have to get some things. I'm sure they'll let me out of the shelter if they know he's in jail. I'll check to make sure he's really there. I have to get us some clean clothes, and some toys for the boys. I want to get my picture albums. He threatened to burn them."

"You want to go to the house?"

"Why not? At least we know he's not going to be there. At least we can know we won't find him hanging from a beam in the living room."

We stopped at a drugstore a few blocks away and called the house. No one was there. We called the jail. They said their records showed that he had been booked but they didn't know for sure whether he'd been bailed out. "Is there any way he can bail out this fast?" Carol asked.

"Only if he uses his own credit card," the man answered.

"I *have* his credit card," Carol said to me after she hung up. "We're so much in debt that I had to take it away from him. Let's just hurry. I hate this! I hate sneaking into my own house this way."

I drove to the house and we held hands going up the walk. "I feel his presence is here, that he's right here seeing me do this," she said, in the dusty, eerie silence of the living room. "Why do I give him so much power?" It's as if he knows whatever I'm thinking, whatever I'm doing. When he was trying to find the children, I thought he had eyes like God, and he would go directly to the school where they were and kidnap them. I had to warn them, 'If you see your father anywhere, run and hide. Don't let him get near you!' Can you imagine telling your children that about their father? Oh God, let's hurry."

She ran from room to room, pulling open drawers, stuffing clothes into paper bags. I stood in the doorway of their bedroom, my heart pounding as I looked at their bed with its tossed covers, at the phone he used to call me. Books were everywhere on the bed—books about how to love better, how to live better, books on the occult, on meditation, books on self-hypnosis for peace of mind. Carol picked up an open book and looked at some words underlined in red. "You can always create your own experience of life in a beautiful and enjoyable way if you keep your love turned on within you—regardless of what other people say or do," she read aloud. She tossed it down in disgust. "He's paying good money for these," she said. She kept blowing her nose.

"Are you crying?"

"No!" she said. "I'm allergic to all this dust."

I walked to the front door, checked the street for his car, and went into the kitchen.

"Look at this," I called to her. On the counter was a row of packages, gift-wrapped. A card was slipped under one of them. Carol opened it and read it aloud: "I have been a brute and I don't deserve you. But I can't live without you and the boys. Don't take that away from me. Try to forgive me." She picked up one of the boxes and then set it down. "I don't believe this," she said. "God, where are the children's picture albums! I can't *find* them." She went running down the hall. In the bathroom, I saw the boys' fish bowl, with their two goldfish swimming in it. The water was clear. Beside the bowl was a piece of notebook paper. Written on it in his hand were the words, *Don't give up, hang on, you have the spirit within you to prevail.*

Two days later he came to my house, bailed out of jail with money his mother had wired. He banged on my front door. He had discovered that Carol had been to the house. "Did you take her there?" he demanded. "*You* wouldn't do that to me, would you?" He stood on the doorstep, gaunt, his hands shaking.

"Was she at the house?" I asked. "I haven't been in touch with her lately."

"Please," he said, his words slurred, his hands out for help. "Look at this." He showed me his arms; the veins in his fore-arms were black-and-blue. "When I saw Carol had been home, I took the money my mother sent me for food and bought three packets of heroin. I wanted to OD. But it was lousy stuff, it didn't kill me. It's not so easy to die, even if you want to. I'm a tough bird. But please, can't you treat me like regular old me; can't you ask me to come in and have dinner with you? I'm not a monster. Can't anyone, *anyone*, be nice to me?"

My children were hiding at the far end of the hall, listening. "Wait here," I said. I went and got him a whole cooked chicken I had. I handed it to him where he stood on the doorstep and stepped back with distaste. Ask him in? Let my children see *this*? Who knew what a crazy man would do? He must have suspected that I knew Carol's exact whereabouts. Whenever I went to visit her at the shelter I took a circuitous route, always watching in my rearview mirror for his blue car. Now I had my tear gas in my pocket; I carried it with me all the time, kept it beside my bed when I slept. I thought of the things in my kitchen: knives, electric cords, mixers, graters, elements which could become white-hot and sear off a person's flesh.

He stood there like a supplicant, palms up, eyebrows raised in hope, waiting for a sign of humanity from me. I gave him what I could—a chicken and a weak, pathetic little smile. I said, dishonestly, "Go home, maybe I can reach her today, maybe she will call you once you get home." He ran to his car, jumped in it, sped off, and I thought, coldly, *Good, I'm rid of him. For now we're safe.* I locked the door with three locks.

Later, Carol found among his many notes to her one which said, "At least your sister smiled at me, the only human thing that happened in this terrible time. I always knew she loved me and was my friend."

He became more persistent. He staked out my house, not believing I wasn't hiding her. "How could I possibly hide her?" I said to him on the phone. "You know I wouldn't lie to you."

"I know you wouldn't," he said. "I trust you." But on certain days I saw his blue car parked behind a hedge a block away, saw him hunched down like a private eye, watching my front door. One day my husband drove away with one of our daughters beside him, and an instant later the blue car tore by. I got a look at him then, curved over the wheel, a madman, everything at stake, nothing to lose, and I felt he would kill, kidnap, hold my husband and children hostages till he got my sister back. I cried out. As long as he lived he would search for her, and, if she hid, he would plague me. He had once said to her (she told me this), "You love your family? You want them alive? Then you'd better do as I say."

On the day he broke the table, after his son's face crumpled in terror, Carol told him to leave. He ran from the house. Ten minutes later he called my sister and said, in the voice of a wild creature, "I'm watching some men building a house, Carol. I'm never going to build a house for you now. Do you know that?" He was panting like an animal. "And I'm coming back for you. You're going to be with me one way or another. You know I can't go on without you."

She hung up and called me. "I think he's coming back to hurt us."

"Then get out of there," I cried, miles away and helpless. "Run!"

By the time she called me again I had the number of the shelter for her. She was at a gas station with her children. Outside were two phone booths—she hid her children in one; she called the shelter from the other. I called the boys at the number in their booth and I read to them from a book called Silly Riddles while she made arrangements to be taken in. She talked for almost an hour to a counselor at the shelter. All the time I was sweating and reading riddles. When it was settled, she came into the children's phone booth and we made a date to meet in forty-five minutes at Sears so she could buy herself some underwear and her children some blue jeans. They were still in their pajamas.

Under the bright fluorescent lights in the department store, we looked at price tags, considered quality and style, while her teeth chattered. Our eyes met over the racks, and she asked me, "What do you think he's planning now?"

My husband got a restraining order to keep him from our doorstep, to keep him from dialing our number. Yet he dialed it, and I answered the phone, almost passionately, each time I heard it ringing, having run to the phone where I had the tape recorder hooked up. "Why is she so afraid of me? Let her come to see me without bodyguards! What can happen? The worst I could do is kill her, and how bad could that be, compared with what we're going through now?"

I played her that tape. "You must never go back," I said. She agreed; she had to. I brought clean nightgowns to her at the shelter; I brought her fresh vegetables, and bread that had substance.

Bard hired a psychic that last week, and went to Las Vegas to confer with him, bringing a $500 money order. When he got home, he sent a parcel to Las Vegas, containing clothing of Carol's and a small gold ring which she often wore. A circular that Carol found later under the bed promised immediate results: *Gold has the strongest psychic power—you can work a love spell by burning a red candle and reciting "In this ring I place my spell of love to make you return to me." This will also prevent your loved one from being unfaithful.*

Carol moved across the street from my house just before Halloween. We devised a signal so she could call me for help in case some maniac cut her phone lines. She would use the antique gas alarm which our father had given to me. It was a loud wooden clacker which had been used in the war. She would open her window and spin it. I could hear it easily. I promised her that I would look out of my window often and watch for suspicious shadows near the bushes under her windows. Somehow, neither of us believed he was really gone. Even though she had picked up his wallet at the morgue, the wallet he'd had with him while he breathed his car's exhaust through a vacuum cleaner hose, thought his thoughts, told himself she didn't love him and so he had to do this and do it now, even though his ashes were in the dumpster, we felt that he was still out there, still looking for her.

Her sons built a six-foot-high spider web out of heavy white yarn for a decoration, and nailed it to the tree in her front yard. They built a graveyard around the tree, with wooden crosses. At their front door they rigged a noose, and hung a dummy from it. The dummy, in their father's old blue sweatshirt with a hood, swung from the rope. It was still there long after Halloween, still swaying in the wind.

Carol said to me, "I don't like it, but I don't want to say anything to them. I don't think they're thinking about him. I think they just made it for Halloween, and they still like to look at it."

# Tell Me Your Secret

THE TIME WAS THE FIFTIES and everything we young women did was fraught with danger. We could get pregnant, we could get raped, we could get lost, we could get seduced, our boyfriends could beg us to iron all their shirts for a year and then not marry us after all. We couldn't get diaphragms without a doctor's appointment but couldn't ask to be fitted for one unless we were about to be married. If we, somehow—heaven forbid—became pregnant, we'd heard that Puerto Rico was the only place we could get an abortion that wouldn't kill us. We were suspected of lascivious behavior as a matter of fact: the campus dress code was rigid and demanded that we not wear shorts more than one inch above the knee, and then only under a non-transparent raincoat, and only for essential sporting events. The dorm mothers rushed around the lounges where we met our young men, ordering us to keep "all four feet on the floor at all times." And of course no men, not even our fathers, were allowed into our dorm rooms.

Those of us who aspired to education learned soon enough that the college administrators at our Florida university were seriously unwilling to give graduate fellowships or teaching assistantships to women, convinced as they were that we'd run off and get married and that men were better risks and more deserving in every case.

Our mothers let us know they hoped for the best, especially that we would be engaged before graduation since afterward, because we'd all be elementary school teachers, the chances of our meeting marriageable men would be negligible. Our fathers, knowing how men are, feared the worst, that we would lose our virginity before being spoken for, but none of them—being men themselves—ever talked to us face-to-face about their concerns.

In spite of all this, I kept humming along in a little cocoon of self-direction, certain that none of society's prescriptions for me were going to affect the outcome of my future. I would get a fellowship if I wanted one, a husband and babies in the right order if I wanted them, and no one I didn't want to get my virginity would get it. I would stay as innocent as I wanted to be for as long as I wanted to be.

An event that upset my grip on this blind certainty happened on a Saturday in the month of May, just before final exams of my junior year. I was in my dorm room ironing a dotted-Swiss pink party dress with fitted bodice and scoop neck and a little white bow at its center. I had just come back from town where I'd bought pink leather flats to go with my dress, and I'd also had my hair cut short so that—with just a toss of my fingers—curls would shimmer all over my head. I was twenty years old and as pretty as I would ever be in this life.

Tonight, in the woods at the edge of town, there would be a party at the home of my psychology professor—Barton Flack, a bearded and attractive man, who—in the classroom—sat on the edge of his desk, tapping his shined loafers against the wooden desk-edge as he lectured. He was famous for inventing a board game that was selling out all over the country and making him a millionaire. With the proceeds, Barton (as he asked us to address him in the interests of equality) had built a modern glass and wood house deep in a forest of Florida pines, with bedrooms separate from the house and ringing the living area like a circle of motel rooms. (He raised his brows suggestively when he described these rooms to the girls who hung around his desk after class.)

He had intimated all semester that when school was out, he'd throw a party like none other and a couple of his selected favorites would be invited to meet some mystery guests, friends of his from the intellectual and art worlds who would surely raise a few hairs on our heads.

Iconoclast that he was, he still had to get around authoritarian rule: girls had to be back in the dorms by curfew. He had to figure out how we could spend the night at his place. We told him we lived under a microscope: each time we left for the evening we were required to sign out on a card kept in a box at the reception desk. We had to state our destination, the name of our companion(s), and our expected time of return. When we came back (if we had the good fortune not to get seduced and left for dead in the lime quarry) we had to certify and initial our time of return.

Barton arranged a deception for me and another student of his by inveigling a couple of his women friends to pretend they were our "aunts" who would appear before the dorm mothers and testify in writing that they were our relatives and were taking us off campus for a night of wholesome and purely educational activities. The opera, perhaps. The other girl, Diane Weinberger, who also lived in my dorm, had agreed to cooperate in the plot. She was not my friend, this short, plain, ordinary-looking girl who never wore makeup, who wore glasses, who was a math major, and who had the distinct look of a lesbian about her (or so some said; I had no experience with lesbians, so left it to those who knew better). Barton seemed to admire her serious demeanor, her powerful mind, and her indifferent dress—she seemed an iconoclast also—at a time when there weren't many around who were girls.

As I prepared for the party, ironing my dress and packing a small overnight case with clothes for the next day, my roommate, Flora Lu Matterfield, sat like a hippopotamus on her bed wearing her elastic chin-lift device, and watched me with a look of despair on her face.

"Honey bun, I'm worried about you, going to that man's house for the night, with God knows what's going to happen out there in the woods. You know that man has a reputation! He knows female psychology, he's famous for it, so that's why he can convince you you're going out there for some so-called party when he could be planning to sell you down the river into white slavery. Otherwise why wouldn't he want to get you back here safe and sound by curfew?" Her mouth, held in an unnatural position by the elastic straps, caused her to speak as if she were under water .

"Parties in the real world don't even get started till around midnight, Flora Lu. How can I expect him—the host—to deliver me back here by curfew?"

"Well, if they find your body in the swamp," Flora Lu said lugubriously, "I refuse to testify in court and say I warned you. I won't muddy your name. I'll just pretend I never saw you pack your little pink lacy nightgown in that little case. I didn't see a thing."

"It's not lace. It's cotton-flannel, Flora Lu."

"In the dark, who will know the difference?"

Flora Lu was frowning and mumbling to herself and leafing through *Bride's Magazine* and I was putting the finishing touches on my dress when the room buzzer sounded. I went to the intercom and buzzed back.

"Special Delivery for Franny at the front desk."

"I'll be right down." I tried to imagine who would send me a Special Delivery. Maybe I was being notified that I'd won a poetry contest I'd entered. Maybe it was from Ted, a young man with whom I'd been pen pals for years. He liked to shock me by sending bizarre packages. Once, after he visited Italy, he sent me little sealed bottles of polluted water from the Venetian Canals.

The girl at the desk handed me a blue airmail envelope, with scrawls all over it that said: "RUSH! PRIVATE! URGENT! PERSONAL!" The return address was from Billy Carp, a childhood friend of mine who still lived in Brooklyn, where I'd grown up. I took the letter upstairs and read the first sentence: "Dear Franny, I saw your grandmother this morning and I will see her again this afternoon." This puzzled me. Why would Billy see her in any case? She was 87 years old; I hadn't seen her in several years, myself. She was in a nursing home, paralyzed by a stroke. My aunt lived nearby and visited her daily. My aunt and Billy's mother were friends, but Billy was at Brooklyn College and wouldn't normally be seeing my grandmother. "No one here wanted to tell you this, but I feel it's my duty as your friend to be sure you know the truth. Your parents have always protected you from the realities of life, whereas my mother always let me have it right up front, from the day my father died when I was twelve to the lovers my mother brought home when I was in high school."

Feeling alarmed, I turned the page over and read the end of the letter.

"She was old anyway, and her life wasn't worth much. Don't lose too much sleep over this. It's the way of the world. Love from your good friend, Billy." Now I scanned the letter in panic, looking for the operational phrase, which finally I found. "Your grandmother died today of massive blood loss from bleeding ulcers. Your folks didn't plan to tell you this till after you finished your final exams. I went with my mother and your aunt to the hospital this morning, and we'll be going to the Jewish Funeral Home this afternoon."

I sat down on my bed.

"Honey, you're white as a ghost. Tell Flora Lu what's wrong."

"My grandmother died."

"Lord a mercy," she said. She put down her magazine. "Well, I guess you can just forget your little party now." She stared at my face and then pulled off her chin-lift device. "Honey, you stay here with me and I'll take good care of you. We'll light a little candle and pray together for her precious soul that just passed on."

I left my room, walked out the back door of the dorm and followed the path out to the miniature golf course. I looked up: trees, sky. The great glory of Nature. Death. Death was part of Nature. I knew I wasn't feeling the proper emotions. This was bad news. My mother's mother dead. Someday it would be my mother, then me. I kept pushing myself into different slots, trying to know what to feel. Where were my tears? Where was my heart? Why wasn't I crying? Why, in fact, was I thinking about my pink dress and worrying that now I probably wouldn't get to wear it tonight? I suddenly remembered my father's older sister, my aunt who had committed a terrible crime in our family. I'd heard her black heart cursed many times: "Did you know that the night her mother died your Aunt Ruth actually went to a party?" It was the worst that could be said about her—this horror she had committed, this taint she had brought down on the family. Privately I had always thought it wasn't such a bad thing to do: if you had a party to go to and someone died, why not go to your party? The dead wouldn't particularly care, would they? If they loved you, they'd want you to go on having your life.

I definitely wanted to have my life. In fact, I had a feeling that some part of it was actually going to start tonight, at the party. My anger swung toward Billy. Why hadn't he minded his own business? Now I had an obligation to feel bad. I'd have to call home and argue with my parents, blaming them for treating me like a child. I would get upset, I might cry, I'd lose my dreamy party rhythm (I was losing it already), and I'd be too far gone to think of going anywhere.

Maybe I could just pretend the letter hadn't arrived. It was just a matter of information. Why not imagine I simply didn't know about this death and continue to feel happy? I could go back upstairs and choose which necklace to wear to decorate the scoop neckline of the dress—a small, final act of grace I had been looking forward to all day. If only I hadn't told Flora Lu!

I looked up at the dorm windows and I felt that, against my will, the entire landscape of my world had changed. I was now obligated to think about the meaning of death, the short span of man's life, how life was, as we had learned in Shakespeare class, "a walking shadow, a poor player that struts and frets his hour upon the stage and then is heard no more... a tale told by an idiot, full of sound and fury, signifying nothing...."

Right now I was supposed to be shedding tears, trying to remember little things about my grandmother and starting to miss her. I also should probably be thinking about God and his role in all this, if there was a God and if he had a role. This was all very far from my present interests. Light years away. The deeper meanings of life seemed totally irrelevant to me. Why should I waste my time on such useless pondering?

At 8 p.m., as soon as the buzzer rang in my room, I hurried out with my little suitcase despite Flora Lu's pronouncement that I was bound to go to hell for this. The "aunt" who came to sign me out at the front desk wore an emerald-green satin dress, gold earrings shaped like serpents, and sling-back suede high-heels. As I came down the ramp into the lobby, she teetered toward me in little mincing steps because of the narrowness of her dress and held her arms out to embrace me. As she hugged me to her visibly pointed breasts, waves of her perfume blazed into my eyes and made them tear. Since she apparently had already completed her paperwork with the dorm mother, she put her arm around me, took my overnight case in her free hand, and walked me toward the door. Just then Diane Weinberger arrived in the lobby and I saw a woman in a navy blue suit— carrying an alligator handbag— rise from a chair and walk toward her. Another embrace took place: Diane stood like a stick of concrete while the woman exclaimed about how pretty she looked. (Diane was dressed in brown corduroy pants and a man's plaid shirt.)

"Shall we go?" my new friend advised. She led me out the door. I gave myself up to her, let her put me into her red sports car, let her speed away into the night with me, and allowed her to deliver me into the labyrinth of the professor's dark woods.

* * *

All of the guests at the party, standing in the circular, brightly lit living room, holding drinks and paper plates of food, were reflected back upon themselves from the great panes of glass that looked into the black forest. It seemed a scene from a horror movie: while they were all blindly chattering away and eating hors d'oeuvres, the woods were closing in on them like an iron trap and would shortly devour them.

I would surely be afraid to live here myself, walking alone through the house at night, reading unprotected in the glare of the bright lights, while outside, surrounding me, the mysterious woods hid whatever eyes might be looking in at me.

Barton had furnished his new house with orange furniture—strangely shaped plastic orange tables, orange canvas cloth laid over black metal chair frames, orange Chinese paper lanterns, orange ash trays. My professor circulated among his guests; he was smoking a cigar. His shoes were especially highly polished, his beard neatly trimmed, pointed and giving him a little air of the devil. He put his arm around me and told me I looked beautiful.

Leading me around the circular room, he introduced me to his friends: a South American diplomat (a tall, hairy, bearlike man with a sweet smile), an actress (the woman in green satin who was my "aunt"), a poet, a playwright, the owner of an alligator farm, a professor of philosophy.

Diane Weinberger stood under an orange paper lantern talking to the diplomat; her hands hung at her sides, holding neither cup nor plate. The man kept offering his plate to her, and finally he picked up a shrimp wrapped in bacon and popped it into her mouth. When she had swallowed, she opened her mouth for another.

Music was playing: Yma Sumac singing one of her weird and unearthly songs—she was a woman whose voice had an uncanny range, from bass to highest soprano. I'd heard her on the radio—she gave me the feeling that if I listened to her too long I would be driven insane.

I told myself that I was finally at the professor's party, the party I had so badly wanted to attend and for which I had prepared for days. The party that promised so much and for which I had betrayed the moral teachings of my upbringing and made an enemy of my roommate. Since I was here, I was duty-bound to enjoy myself. And if Diane Weinberger—a girl as Jewish as I was—could eat shrimp and bacon, so could I. I piled my plate high. I ate at least a dozen of these delicacies; they were delicious, the white chewy forbidden shrimp circled by the fried, crisp, salty flesh of pig.

There was dancing and drinking long into the night. No one danced with me, but I sat in an orange chair and watched those who did. Barton and the actress-in-satin moved their bodies together in ways I didn't know was possible. At some point, during a lull in the music, my professor brought out his board game and we all sat down on the orange rug in a circle to play his invention: "Tell Me Your Secret."

There was the traditional gameboard and the conventional dice to throw. Unlike Monopoly that frequently sent you to jail, this game had instructions on the board to "Go Back To Your Mother's Womb" or "Confess In The Palace of Dreams" or "Take A Card From The Treasure Cave."

The cards were dangerous as quicksand: they required that each player tell a secret. "Tell your most embarrassing memory." "Tell about the time you stole something from a store." "Tell about the night you saw your parents in bed together." "Tell about the first time you played doctor as a child." Each time a member of the party hesitated, Barton would pour his guest another glass of champagne, and the others would urge him on. There was much laughter and then, eventually—a secret was blurted out, after which there was even more laughter. The things I heard were shocking to me; I felt I needed a long time to think about each confession, to understand what its impact on the person might have been. Everyone else, though, would listen to a confession, laugh knowingly, and then look up, ready and waiting for the next revelation.

My turn was coming up soon. The South American diplomat told of how, when he was fourteen, he had had sex with his cousin, a woman of twenty-five. Diane Weinberger revealed that her older brother used to read dirty stories to her and then gave her a nickel to rub his penis "till it popped and the scum came out." She stated this with cool satisfaction. Then she admitted she didn't think any man could ever excite her as much as her brother had in their youth.

How could I play this game? What comparable thing could I say—that I had once read a scene in a novel called *God's Little Acre* about a girl getting spanked with a hairbrush and it interested me unduly so that I read it over several times and still remembered it? Or that I had taken a quarter from the dresser of one of my girlfriends and hid it in my sock when I was eleven years old? I began to think of Flora Lu with longing; oh to be back in my dorm room, safe under the blankets, the lights long out after the more-than-reasonable curfew, which was designed for my own good!

Now some truth would be extracted from me and transform me in the minds of others—and even my own—into a different person. In the next few moments, I would lose my privacy forever.

The dice were put in my hands by my professor. "Have courage!" he whispered to me. "The truth will set you free."

I cast the dice. I moved my game piece. I chose my card and read it.

"Tell the thing you are most ashamed of."

I looked around the circle at the faces of the guests who now seemed to wait in judgement for my confession. Everyone's eyes were upon me, everyone's mouths seemed loose and limp, hanging open with lascivious hunger.

"I came to this party..." I said, "even though I just learned today...I came here even though...my grandmother died." I waited for the glass walls of the professor's house to implode, for one of the glass shards to pierce my heart. I thought of my mother, broken-hearted at home, and of my father, who would die of grief to see me here, besotted with champagne and fattened to bursting with bacon and shrimp.

"How old was she?" the actress asked.

"She was eighty-seven."

"Oh well. That doesn't count then, you can't be guilty about that!" she said. "She lived long enough. It has to be something you're really ashamed of."

"It counts." Barton defended me. He came and knelt beside me and put his arm around my shoulder. "She is ashamed. That's what Franny has to tell you. That's what you have to accept. The rules of the game are that you can't challenge what someone feels is her truth."

I passed the dice to the next person in the circle. She tossed them and I was forgotten. I excused myself and went to find the orange bathroom where all the little orange soaps were in the shapes of women's breasts. I wanted to cry, but I had had too much champagne to be able to get near the place where my tears resided.

* * *

It was nearly dawn and I was half-asleep in a chair when the actress offered to lead me to my guest room for the night. Just as we had heard, the bedrooms were separate from the house, arranged in a row of motel-like rooms, their walls, like those in the house, made entirely of glass that looked into the woods on two sides. I went into the bathroom which adjoined the guest room on the other side and locked both doors in order to get undressed out of view of the windows, to put on my cotton-flannel nightgown and brush my teeth, like a good girl. Through the door I could hear the voices of Diane Weinberger and the South American diplomat. He had a deep booming laugh, like rolling thunder. Her laugh was high and whiny, but full of a strange, giddy joy. Soon they stopped talking and began gasping and guffawing breathlessly as if they were tickling one another.

I got into bed and shut off the bedside lamp as fast as possible. With the light off, I could see a few feet into the woods by the glow of light coming from the next room. The pine trees were enormous, weighted down by Spanish moss that waved in the wind like witches' hair.

From the other side of the wall I could hear the noises of Diane Weinberger and the hairy man. I could hear the bedsprings rumble, I could hear her high cries and his low groans. I listened, totally alert, for a very long time. Holding onto the sides of my bed, I traveled with them on their ride, their slow, deliberate journey over the twists and turns of the tracks, inching up the roller coaster to the screaming, blinding pitch of sensation. After their last screams, someone turned off the light in their room, plunging the woods into darkness.

I lay there, hot in my bed under the sheet, smelling the scent of sawdust from the new wood flooring. Heat lightning flashed in the sky and the rumble of thunder vibrated through the room. With every flash of light, I thought I saw a face looking in the huge window. I begged myself to go to sleep.

Through the glass I watched the full moon riding under and over the blowing storm clouds till it was buried in blackness. Again I saw a face at my window. The door, which had no lock on it, opened slowly and Barton Flack's voice whispered my name.

"Franny? Are you awake? There's a big storm blowing in. It can get pretty fierce out here; I didn't want you to be afraid."

"I'm not afraid," I said.

My professor came and sat down on the edge of my bed. He was wearing some kind of loose caftan; he found my hand and began to stroke my arm.

"This has been a very strange night for you, Franny," he said. "I know you've been very, very careful in your life so far. I just want to tell you—there's no prize for being careful." He reached up and touched my face. Then he leaned forward, cupped my head in his hands and kissed my lips very gently. "You could come into bed with me and my friend," he said. "We could ride out the storm together. It could be one of our secrets."

He waited for my answer. After a great burst of lightning, the moon appeared again in the sky. My white-haired grandmother was by now deep under the ground, cold as stone, still as stone, giving up her soft flesh to the history of the earth. "The sun shall not smite her by day, nor the moon by night," I heard in my mind. My own history was just beginning. How short a time lay ahead to be under sun and moon.

My professor was standing now beside my bed, his hand extended to me. "Come," he invited me. "We will enjoy the night."

After a moment, I let him pull me to my feet.

# Night Stalker

*N*IGHT STALKER. *Night Walker.*

The anchormen outdo themselves giving the murderer poetic names. One news reporter calls him *The Valley Intruder.* No one can agree on his essence other than to warn that he is dangerous. "Light up and lock up," the police chief advises. "And get yourself a big barking dog."

That's her trouble—Berry still has Sylvie's dogs at his house and won't give them back to her. Her mistake was to let Berry train them for quail hunting and now he says he has too much invested in them to give them back to her. "If you just want to rub up against something soft—or is it something hard?—you can get that anywhere, as you have demonstrated so well," he said last week in a flat, ugly tone of voice. "But the dogs and me—we share an art form."

Sylvie buys a cowbell at the flea market in the Rose Bowl and hangs it inside the back door of the house she rented when she moved out of Berry's house. She forgets it's there, though, and every time she goes out to feed her cats, the big square bell swings against the door with a wild dissonant clang and shocks her.

She keeps a piece of paper on her refrigerator, fastened to the door with a magnet shaped like a pair of kissing lips, and whenever she thinks of a killer's descriptive name, she writes it down. "Son of Sam," "Zodiac Killer," "Skid Row Slasher," "Hillside Strangler."

The reason the media can't settle on a name for the Stalker is that he doesn't seem to have any special needs—he kills everyone, men and women, young and old. The other psychos had had definite preferences: girls with dark hair parted down the middle, derelicts clutching wine bottles, hookers, hitchhikers. The Night Stalker/Walker doesn't give Sylvie a chance to wrap her fear around anything specific. He seems to want to be democratic in providing his services.

At the beginning of his rampage, the police announced he was out to get women living alone. They said his mode of entry was through open windows in dimly lit yellow houses without fenced yards. They said there were indications that he liked to observe women watching television late at night before he struck. Sylvie decides the police are talking about her on the news, and in a minute will give out her name and address. That's her exactly, down to the "dimly lit." She now lives in a little rented yellow house which has no outside light, no fenced yard (if she had one, she'd have bought a German shepherd and a Doberman right away—to make up for Franco and Chumley, her dogs which Berry won't give back to her).

And she always watches television late at night. With no one to talk to, the television is her main human connection. It doesn't matter what comes on the screen—David Letterman giving people coins to put in the candy machines, Rumpole of the Bailey mumbling under his breath, the moose on the wall at Fawlty Towers coming off the hook and hitting John Cleese on the head. Even Captain Kirk, in his straight-backed moral certainty, is oddly reassuring. When finally she has to go to bed, when her eyes won't stay open, she locks the doors and windows and says goodbye to her cats, just in case. "I surrender myself into the arms of Jesus," she tells them, kissing them both between the ears. She thinks anyone's arms would be comforting, under the circumstances.

Driving to work she hears on the radio that one of the Stalker's surviving victims has revealed an important fact: the killer has discolored and rotted teeth, widely spaced. Perfect, she thinks, imagining the man leaning over her in bed. She knows just which side he'll be standing on when he comes to her, how he'll blot out the red light from the neon-bright display on her clock. Berry used to keep a shotgun under the bed. She longs not for him but for the highly developed muscles in his arms and for his perfect aim.

On the freeway, on her way to the hospital, she looks into each car that passes her. She believes that if any man glances out the window of his car and smiles at her, she will see at once his rotted, discolored, gapped teeth.

She had just wanted to be easy on herself during the winter. She was the one with the forty-hour job, she was the one tied down, while Berry was off in the woods with her dogs, hopping from one state to another, elk hunting, quail hunting, visiting his Vietnam buddies, hunkering down somewhere for a month while she drove her little Toyota to the lab, put on her lab coat, stuck needles in the tender stomachs of mice, made notations, cleaned up, drove home again, fed the cats and ate alone. Her dogs' big stainless-steel bowls, dented and empty, rolling in the wind against each other outside the back door, caused her more misery than the vacant side of Berry's waterbed.

Now and then she'd get a call from Berry, from some honky-tonk bar in the north, telling her he was making good money acting as a guide to elk-hunters, winning a lot of cash at poker, telling her that the dogs were doing just fine. Several times she was aware he had covered the mouthpiece to say something to someone else. For a long time after she hung up, the sound of pounding music remained in her ears.

Being easy on herself meant giving herself permission to jog with Richard—Dr. Richard Gomber, the man for whom she conducted experiments and did research. Before lunch every day the two of them jogged together around the hospital. They took a convenient path—it made a loop around the cafeteria, the motel-village where families of dying patients lived, the catastrophic illness wing, and the medical records building. Whenever they passed the famous fountain at the entrance to the hospital, droplets of cool water hit her in the face like a vaccine. Sacred water: it flew into the air above the blessed dancing family—a mother, father and child, hands joined in celebration. Health and joy and love—reminders, should anyone passing by forget, of the reasons for wanting to remain alive.

Her chest heaving, her heart pounding, she would forget what was coming till they were right at the hospital entrance where the fountain made its dramatic statement, and then she saw them—sitting on its cold stone rim—a mother and child. Though the people were never the same, they always had the same look about them. The mother sat holding the hand of her bald little son, or her bald little daughter, the two of them taking the air, getting buoyed up, finding courage for going into chemotherapy, or for going home to deal with its effects. Not once did Sylvie ever see a father sitting on the edge of the fountain.

Having children was not something she had thought about much before, but whenever she saw the little five-year-olds sitting on the rounded, mica-sparkled rim of the fountain, she wanted to caress their bald heads, stroke their frightened faces, and rock them in her arms. She began to understand why she didn't care for Berry: he was not a carrier of fine genetic material. She wished she had considered that when she was younger. She would have looked for a man like Richard, whose intelligence illuminated and enlarged all that he touched. A pediatrician for children with leukemia, his job, when he wasn't inserting huge hollow needles into the breastbones of children, was to kill the laboratory mice and see what was going on inside. Her job was to shoot leukemic cells into the mice.

One day in winter, though it was raining, Richard wanted to run. He said he felt unable to face the afternoon's work without his run. He took Sylvie's hand briefly and pulled her into the corridor. They began to run in their white coats through the halls of the hospital. No one suspected an emergency because everything was an emergency here. Their casual hospital had abandoned the idiotic rules of regular hospitals, rules which fussed about children visiting, worried about the spread of germs, detailed to the minute the permitted hours of socializing. At this place there was only one thought beating in the veins of every patient, nurse, doctor, and lab worker: nothing silly mattered, there was no time for silliness.

Therefore the older children were permitted to play music on their tape decks till all hours—the songs of their rock heroes who had energy to spare and whose cries and shouts magically, temporarily, revivified. On that rainy winter afternoon, Sylvie and Richard ran past a room where two spirits were gyrating in their hospital robes, a bald teenage boy and a bald teenage girl, their bony buttocks showing through the openings in their white cotton gowns, their toothpick legs vibrating as they danced.

That night, Richard came home with Sylvie although at his house his wife was keeping his dinner warm, and two children waited for him. It was the same night that Berry's friend Judson came by to borrow some tools and the next time Berry called home, he told Sylvie he didn't want her there when he got back. She tried to explain that she was being easy on herself, that it had been a terrible, lonely winter, but Berry wasn't interested. Actually, she didn't really care that she had to move out. Berry had floated so far away from her, he was like a feathery seed pod; she could hardly focus on him. Besides, she'd always disliked his waterbed. She could never get still in it; it never let her become peaceful and perfectly still while she slept, but always nagged her back to some guarded alertness by its insistent churning restless tides.

Once Sylvie has moved out of Berry's house she imagines she has changed. At the lab, she finds herself staring at her image reflected in the stainless-steel sides of the autoclave, looking like an angel in her white lab coat, injecting the underbellies of the mice that struggle in her hand. She doesn't look like an evil woman. She wonders why people who do what they have to do are considered evil. Is the Night Stalker more evil than she?

When she and Richard jog, whenever they pass a mother and her bald child resting on the rim of the fountain, Richard makes a strange sound—it's almost like a sob. It could be merely an exhalation of exertion, but it recurs each time they see a little child sitting in the rainbow spray of the fountain, and Sylvie understands it's involuntary. He doesn't know he makes the sound. It comes from his soul.

The radio hints that the Stalker does indescribable deeds in the homes of his victims. He enacts rituals; he writes on the walls with blood, he mutilates, sings, chants, hops on one foot like a beheaded chicken while speaking in tongues. The morning paper features a composite drawing of him—a curly-headed, pointy-chinned boy with large, liquid brown eyes. His eyes are like the eyes on paintings of waifs done by commercial artists: grieved and suffering eyes. The police haven't much to go on; they're alerted by a dentist who remembers that such a man has been in his office—a man with stained, rotted, widely gapped teeth. Copies of the man's dental records are sent to thousands of dentists in the city. Sylvie imagines the killer sitting in an air-conditioned office aromatic with peppermint mouthwash; he is racked with pain and is watching a clock (like the one her dentist has in his office) made of silver ball bearings; as each minute passes, a silver ball falls with a noise like a gunshot from one wooden tray into another.

In her yellow unfenced dimly lit house, she gives the killer a better name than anyone has thought of yet. *Night Talker*. He comes at night and he talks. He talks to women and men, to old dying people and young dying children. He tells them dramatic, descriptive, passionate tales of what he has seen on his street, in his home, on his ward, in his ghetto, barrio, town house, mansion. He confides that he considers himself not a murderer but a deliverer from pain. When he finally visits Sylvie with his gun or hatchet or knife, he will want her to remember that he has walked through the halls of her hospital and has seen the sweet skeletal teenagers dancing to Bruce Springsteen's hoarse throbbing encouragements.

Sylvie suspects she is beginning to let go. One of Richard's children, his five-year-old son, has been getting small black and blue marks all over his body. Petechiae. The *sign*. Richard is in bed with her in the yellow house when he tells her this. He tells her this and then leaps out of bed. He finds the cowbell on her kitchen door and rings it over his head. In a fury, he asks her, "Why is the Night Stalker any different from the Stalker in my lab, in my house? Why are you so afraid *here* but not in the lab? Do you think your white coat protects you from anything? Do you think mine protects *me*?" He runs through the house naked, ringing the cowbell. She sees the heavy knob of the ringer shaking in time to his trembling penis.

In the morning, she discovers the teenaged boy, the bald dancing boy, in her lab in his wheelchair. The radio on her shelf is playing loud music and he is watching the mice in their silver cages. With the long thin fingers of his right hand, he is offering a tidbit through the wire grid.

"What's this?" she says, in mock fierceness. "Didn't you see the sign? No feeding the animals in this zoo!"

"Why not?" the boy asks her, turning upon her face his huge blue eyes, radiant and blue as heaven.

*Why not*? She asks herself. She wonders if he wants to know about the experiments, how some mice are being deprived of Vitamin E, how others are being given an all-protein diet.

"They deserve a little fun," he says. He looks like a hundred-year-old man, his bald skull is almost pointy at the top. "Don't you think they ought to have a taste of fudge brownie before they die?" He's not pleading for special favors; there's no hint of self-pity in his remark.

"By all means," she says. "Go right ahead." She takes her grease pencil and makes a mark on the card on the cage where the brownie crumbs are being pushed through the grating. These mice will be unusable in Richard's experiment. They will have to be killed sooner then others, because of their chocolate treat.

A news bulletin on the radio announces the murder of an old woman living alone. The Stalker is suspected.

"Where do you live?" the boy asks her, putting his hand on her white lab coat, just on her hip. She feels a throb in her belly, low down, almost sexual.

"You mean what street?"

"No, I mean, is it a safe place?"

"Well, I hope so. It's just a little yellow house, shaped like a box. I keep the doors locked."

"Do you live alone?"

"Yes, usually."

"You don't think he'd try to come into the hospital, do you?"

"Does that worry you?"

"Sometimes it does," the boy says. "But not much. Do you have a dog?"

"I have two cats. I used to have two dogs, Chumley and Franco, but I don't have them anymore."

"What happened to them?"

"Someone thought he deserved them more than me."

"Did he?"

"I don't think so."

"That's not fair, is it?"

"I guess not," Sylvie says.

"My folks are getting me a dog when I get out of here. If I ever get out."

"Are you counting on that?"

"Not really. How can I?"

Sylvie motions to the cages, full of scrambling white mice, and lets her hand fall. There are no promises here, either.

"They're going to be looking for me soon," says the boy. "Another bone marrow today. I hate them."

"Is Dr. Gomber your doctor?"

"You mean Richard?"

"Yes. He's really gentle," Sylvie says.

"It doesn't matter," the boy says. "It hurts like hell anyway." He wheels his chair around, expertly, and waves at Sylvie as he rolls into the corridor.

"Come back anytime," she offers. "Bring me a brownie, too."

The Stalker has killed again. This time he shot the man in the house and raped the woman. Having a man in the house is no guarantee of anything. Sylvie locks her doors at night and kisses her cats goodbye, as usual. Instead of imagining Berry's strong muscles, or Richard's pained sweet face, she begins to imagine the boy in the wheelchair sitting beside her bed all night, keeping vigil. He is so serene, so resigned, so death-like, his head so much like a skull already, that he seems to pave the way for her, prepare her for the transition to being one of the Stalker's victims. She imagines the three of them could have a little visit first. They'd talk about suffering. Fear, panic, anger, neglect, unfairness. It would be quite a night. The boy in the wheelchair could talk about tolerating pain, the tricks he has learned, and reassure the Stalker that the dentist isn't so bad, nothing there coming even close to a bone marrow. And even a bone marrow passes, and you live through it. You live through everything till finally you quit, and when you quit nothing hurts anymore.

It's almost a jolly thought, and helps her to go to sleep. Richard's son hasn't got leukemia; it's something else, which can be fixed. Sylvie is ashamed of her disappointment. Somehow she'd painted for herself a delicious scene, in one of those sleepless cavernous nights of listening for noises outside the window—Richard's son would die, his wife would throw herself from the roof of the catastrophic illness wing, and Richard would marry Sylvie. They would have a child, and the three of them would dance for joy like the figures in the sculpture on the stone fountain.

The identity of the Stalker is made known at the exact end of summer, on Labor Day weekend. His face is in the Saturday morning paper, front page, he has been identified by fingerprints and soon they hope to catch him. He is not who she thought he was. His face is wrong; he is not a waif, he is not a sufferer, he is not a deliverer. He is an inflictor of horror, and has darkness written all over him. She is horrified that she imagined it would be interesting to talk to him.

It's been a long, hot weekend, full of the deadness that comes with holidays during which there is no formal activity. No work, no mail delivery, nothing to do. Richard is in Santa Barbara with his family. The smog is heavy, Sylvie's eyes burn. She can barely keep her eyes open as she reads the newspaper. She is so bored that she reads through all the want ads: business opportunities, personals, lost birds, dogs for sale. Sylvie decides to buy a dog. She makes a quick phone call to a man in the Valley who raises basset hounds. "I'm coming," she tells him, and her blood is up. She's grateful for purpose. While she puts on lip gloss in the bathroom, she turns on the radio and hears the triumphant voice of the newsman with his bulletin: someone has hit the Stalker on the head with a pipe and subdued him. He's caught! They've got him! She sinks down on the edge of the bathtub, feeling tearful. She realizes that she doesn't need the bother of a dog now, the house-training, the puppy cries, the barking, the fleas. But she's counting on going out the door, getting into the car, turning the key in the ignition.

As Sylvie unlocks her car, a woman from the house next door, who is standing in the street, runs up to her and hugs her.

"Thank God!" she cries. "Now we can open our windows! Now we can sleep at night!" Several children pour out of another small house and begin lighting fireworks. A celebration of the strangest sort begins to develop. Men come out into the street, some carrying beer cans, and gather, talking about the details of the capture, the arrest. The sound of an electric guitar bursts forth from a garage, filling the air with music. Strangers are congratulating one another as if the angel of death has passed over all of them.

The basset hound she chooses has ears which sweep the ground, and huge flat splayed feet. He has the kind of eyes she wants to see: sweet, limpid, loving. She holds him against her breast as if he is an infant. He comes with everything—shots, collar, leash, bag of puppy food, a huge plastic dish with a family of basset hounds painted on it.

She drives to the hospital with the puppy on her lap, overriding the sense of cliché she feels. The puppy won't stay in the carton. She laughs aloud at the feel of his paws dancing on her lap, tickling her thighs through her skirt.

Hardly anyone is on duty today. She parks in the visitors' lot and walks the dog to the fountain. Sitting on the stone rim with him, she holds him into the rainbow spray, and he bites at the droplets of water, barking hysterically.

Then she carries the puppy into the catastrophic illness wing, where she looks into each room till she finds the dancing boy who brought brownies to the mice. "Hi, I have a surprise for you," she says.

Slowly, he moves himself to a sitting position with the controls of the electric bed. He takes his headphones off his ears.

"I can't keep him here, you know," he says regretfully, taking the puppy in his thin arms and closing his eyes as the dog licks his face. "You can't really do this, you know. Even here there are rules."

"I need him for protection, I'm not giving him to you," Sylvie says. "I know the rules. This is just a visit."

"It's been a boring weekend," the boy says, stroking the puppy's ears.

"It's been deadly," Sylvie agrees.

# The Cleopatra Birds

I MET MY HUSBAND DAVY in Bill's Fish Fry where I was a waitress. He was frying fish when I first saw him, and the way he held the fillets, white and cold in the flat of his hand just before he slid them into the lumpy batter, made me want to marry him. He had a beard like a lumberjack and forearms like Popeye. The waitresses had to wear little pink nets over their hair, but Davy's beard just hung down over the food like the wisdom of Moses. Twice a day when he went on his breaks I had to fry the fish myself. I tried to emulate him: I tried not to hold the fish between my two fingers three feet from my body or hold my breath as I swished it through the bubbly flour mixture and then flopped it down into the boiling yellow oil. I especially tried not to jump back to escape being scalded. I wanted to live up to some kind of image that I imagined he'd admire.

I thought Davy was a student at Western Arts like the rest of us who worked there. I asked him what he was majoring in when there was a lull in fish to fry. He was wearing a tall white chef's hat, so at first I didn't realize how far his hairline had receded. "I'm majoring in fish," he said, and he chopped off the head and tail of an Orange Roughy with a flash of his cleaver.

"I'm majoring in African Dance," I said, though he hadn't asked me.

"What does that mean? You put on war paints and whoop it up?"

The first night I went out with him he took me to a western bar; as we danced he said that when I held my arms back and my chest forward, I looked like one of those beautiful women on the prow of a great ship. I felt as if I had been on the high seas a long time. When he came toward me I had the sweetest sensation that I was floating softly into my safe harbor. He gave me information about himself, which he thought would help his case; he had saved over $15,000 from working as a meat cutter at The Pantry for two years. (The jagged scars on his hands were not from sharp blades, he told me, but from the dull ones.) He could always earn good money by fishing or carpentry, and he would always be happy to cook dinner for me because he was a first-rate cook. By the time we got married I had already come to terms with the fact that he was not, and never would be, a student; I thought I was tired of education. All those pages, read and memorized, and what to show for it? The only thing that made me feel engaged was the movement of my feet in a hard rhythm on the surface of the earth.

We bought a fixer-upper house on a hill in the city of Vulture Rock in a neighborhood where there were gang wars every night. We could hear gunshots after dinner whenever we sat out on the wooden porch to watch the sunset. Vulture Rock itself was a hundred-foot-high boulder shaped like a bird's head just at the edge of the freeway. The bird's face was pockmarked from daily peppering by rifle bullets. Davy and I talked about fencing in the front yard and buying some ducks.

In the backyard Davy began to build an aviary because he wanted to raise quail and doves to use in training a bird dog to hunt. I was busy writing my dissertation on the uses of African music in fertility rites and now and then I would look up from my keyboard and hear the sounds of Davy hammering outside.

When I finished the rough draft of my dissertation, we went to a bird show out at the fairgrounds to celebrate. Hundreds of families milled around examining the latest in incubators and brooding boxes. All the men looked like Davy, with heavy upper bodies, tight jeans below, and expensive leather boots on their feet. Their wives were young, but had small pot bellies, and usually had several children tugging on their shirts. Davy looked like he had been born in the fairgrounds. He walked a little ahead of me and stopped at the registration booth to buy $10 worth of raffle tickets for a $3000 parrot they were giving away. He also bought me a jar of pickled quail eggs for a snack. The eggs were the size of large olives with surprisingly orange yolks. They were sour. I felt it was dangerous to swallow one of them, although I did. As we wandered through the display areas filled with cages, Davy stopped every few feet and bent over to exchange looks with some bird. He rested his hands on his thighs and stared, eye to black eye. In every cage the frightened birds ruffled their feathers and dipped their nervous heads. Their black eyes snapped meanly at Davy as he inspected them. I didn't really like birds; they were very stupid, and all their decisions were instinctive. Davy's face was full of concentration as he knelt to examine the pair of Valley quail he wanted to buy. He seemed to want to make friends with the birds, which I knew was completely impossible. They knew it, too. Only Davy didn't know it. He leaned close to the wire and made cooing noises.

Then he wrapped his arm around my legs and tugged me down. "See if you like them. If you do, we'll get this pair." I knelt down, too, and pretended to make friends, the way you do with a puppy, but the birds just gave me back their black cold stares and one of them dropped a pellet of excrement into the straw.

"Any pair you want is fine with me."

My main thought was that I was glad Davy would have something with which to occupy himself while I was busy leading my life. I still had to take my orals and give a dance performance. I had two years to finish up if I needed to take that long. Davy said there was no rush.

A woman with a cigarette-hoarse voice started reading off the raffle winners over the PA system. It was an endless list; the Wild Game Bird Association was giving away a hundred minor prizes as well as the rare parrot. I asked Davy for some change and left him standing hopefully with the crowd near the raffle table while I went to buy a Coke at the concession stand. Soft drinks cost a dollar. A tall man in a cowboy hat saw that I didn't have enough money and he bought me the Coke. I thanked him. Just looking at him, I knew what he was like: how he talked, what he said to his wife, what kind of TV programs he watched, how he made love. It was cold in the big hanger-like building. I saw the doorway opening out to the parking lot, thirty feet high and filled with sunshine, and I took my Coke and got myself out of the dim echoing building filled with screaming birds and the hoarse monotonous voice of the prize-announcer.

Davy didn't win the parrot but he won a pair of common Australian finches with orange beaks and orange feet. He came jubilantly to find me, holding the little cardboard box with the birds beating their wings to pieces inside it. I tried not to be led back into the bird house, but Davy wanted to show me a pair of rare birds: the Lady Amhersts. They were a variety of pheasant; the males looked like Egyptian queens, with square-cut hairdos and brilliant bands of jewels across their foreheads. Their tails filled the entire cage.

"I call them the Cleopatra birds," Davy said. "Don't you think they're beautiful?" The mated pair was staring at me with pure hatred.

"In a cold sort of way."

"I think Cleopatra looks like you," Davy said. "They really cost, but I'm going to buy us a pair someday."

J'tumba, the professor at Western Arts who was my dissertation adviser, asked me to tutor her two little girls in English during the summer. She was going back to Africa to see her parents, and her husband, an international businessman, didn't have the time to teach the children who had only recently come to this country and were backward and shy. They hardly knew any English at all. It seemed a good idea. Davy was leaving to spend the summer salmon fishing in Alaska. He could earn as much as $6000 in a good season, enough to keep us for the winter and more. In the spring he would do building and carpentry. He planned to ship home hundreds of pounds of frozen salmon by air freight. Davy had bought a special freezer to keep them in. He had also built a small smoke house, where he would smoke some of the fish for the sake of variety. Before he left, I suggested that we have a house warming and invite some friends of mine over to visit and drink some wine. Davy shrugged to show he would be tolerant of anything I wanted. He considered himself quite content without company. He didn't like to hang out much with people, and he found my friends a little wordy. Corinne was studying the *oud* at Western and Ralph collected African masks and fertility idols. When they came over they liked to get high and talk for hours. Davy was bored with talk. He liked to keep busy, and do things with his hands. He preferred to kid around with animals, and to fry fish. He bought a pedigreed short-haired pointer and trained her to fetch birds. Sometimes I went with him on field trials and watched Davy shoot down pigeons and send the dog to retrieve them. He had very high standards and was very rough with her. More often I stayed home and played African music and danced around our little house, barefooted, making grunting noises like a native, and watching my white toes creeping along the floor as if they were live animals.

For the first two months of summer after Davy left for Alaska, I stayed home with Phyllis, the bird dog, and the quail and Davy's two cats. In the front yard we now had Marvin and Eloise, a pair of mallard ducks who quacked incessantly and left foul smelling droppings all over the wooden steps leading up to the porch. In the daytime I tutored J'tumba's little girls, wiry six- and eight-year-old sisters with frightened brown eyes. Their father dropped them off every morning at the fence, and honked for them every evening. I never got a look at his face, and came to think of him as the silver Mercedes with the loud horn. After our drill sessions, the children colored in their workbooks and I practiced African dance until the dog started to whine with boredom. I was getting very good at a certain upward-thrusting movement of the chest. The little girls played in the yard with the ducks, or in the house with the bird dog. I wasn't allowed to let Phyllis outside; she was too valuable. Davy had said I could bring her out on the porch and use the shock collar on her if she attacked the cats. He wanted her to understand that she could only attack on command. The shock collar had cost $500; at first Davy had made Phyllis wear a dummy collar, just to get her used to the weight of it, and then he put on the real thing. The first time he used it, the dog did a backward somersault, leaping in the air at least three feet. I could see, or thought I could, every hair on her body stand up. Then she lay stunned. Or dead.

"It's not enough voltage to kill her," Davy assured me. "Don't worry."

Every Friday night Davy called me from Alaska. The static was bad, and in the background was music from whatever bar he was calling from. He and the crew from the salmon boat would go onshore every weekend and his buddies would get drunk on beer. I had no idea what Davy did on the weekends. There were single women all over Alaska; all the bartenders I knew who were women had learned to bartend in Alaska.

Our phone conversations were awkward. I asked him how many salmon he had caught. He asked me how Phyllis was, and inquired after the cats and ducks. I told him a skunk had been in the yard one night and the ducks had made a terrible racket and scared the skunk away, but the smell had been awful. My life, when described that way by phone, seemed empty and terrible. I always assured Davy that I didn't mind at all that he had gone away for three months, but when I hung up the phone one Friday night, I kicked his dog, and then went into my bedroom to cry. I opened a bottle of wine after that and drank the whole thing. Then I heard the commotion in the yard and looked out and saw the white back of the skunk shining in the moonlight and ran to Davy's closet to get out his shotgun. It was in a wooden crate, and when I opened the crate I found a pair of pantyhose, not my size or color, and some magazines with names like *Instructor in Lust* and *Peeping Toms*.

When the silver Mercedes came by on Monday, I went out to the fence to get the little girls myself. Whenever I had talked to African students at Western Arts, they had always admired my blond hair. The night before I had used a lemon rinse to highlight the gold color. J'tumba's husband was so black he shone. The whiteness of his teeth hurt my eyes, strained as they were from too much crying and sensitive from too much wine. His face hung in the window like a dark moon as the girls got out of the back of the car. We exchanged some comments on how well they were doing. They ran up the driveway and started to chase the ducks around the yard.

"When is J'tumba coming back?" I asked, tossing my hair.

"Not soon," he said.

I waited for him to drive off. He just lowered the window a little by pressing a button.

"My husband is fishing in Alaska," I said. "He's hardly getting anything for the salmon this year because of botulism that showed up in one of the packing plants. It only happened to some of the cans; two little holes got punched in the lids, and let the botulism grow. Four people died, so the price of salmon is way down this summer."

"So is the price of gold."

"I hope to visit Africa someday," I said. "I'd like to dance there. I've learned many of your people's dances at Western Arts." I knew he had once been a professor, like his wife, though now he was a very rich businessman.

"I'd like to see you do them."

"Good. Why not come in tonight when you pick up the girls?"

"I'd like to do that," he said in his deep and cultured voice. "I will in fact do just that."

The children wouldn't or couldn't tell me his African name; they said he called himself Philip since he'd come to this country. They did very little reading or spelling for me. I was too restless to listen to them. Instead they helped me to clean the house and bake *b'stilla*, a Moroccan chicken pie. They brushed butter on fifteen sheets of filo dough and sprinkled sugar and cinnamon onto the scrambled eggs we mixed with the slices of chicken. Though it was forbidden, I put Phyllis out in the backyard where she growled menacingly at me and then began to throw herself against the wire mesh of the aviary, snapping her jaws at the doves and the quail and the finches and fixing them with her red-rimmed eyes as the birds fluttered wildly between perches, their feathers flying, their wings dancing in panic. I closed the door and turned my back on them, having important things to attend to.

By the time Philip came back, I had an African drum solo on the stereo, I had incense burning to cover the smell of the duck shit, and I had called Ralph and Corinne to let them know I was coming down with a cold to forestall any unexpected visits.

During dinner, Philip and I sat at opposite ends of the long table like a king and queen, and his children passed the wine bottle back and forth between us. When I stood up to get dessert from the kitchen, I felt I had not left my seat but that a servant had risen from my place to serve us. Philip's curved white smile, against the dark curtain behind him, was like a brilliant crescent moon rising in my mind.

We sat for a while in the living room, among Davy's stuffed and mounted chukar birds, his stretched rattlesnake skin, and his pair of rubber waders, which stood with their cuffs drooping over at the end of the bookcase. Across the room the gold chain of Philip's pocket watch hung gracefully across the dark striped vest of his suit. I invited him out to the front porch, where we sat close together on dusty chairs looking at the chiseled planes of Vulture Rock. He told me the long story of his tribal history, and of the suffering of his noble ancestors. His children fell asleep sucking on ice cubes, and we carried them into my bedroom and laid them down gently on the rumpled blankets. He asked me to dance for him. He waited, drinking wine, while I put on a shift of painted black and white cloth. Then I danced my dance across the living room, heaving my chest upward like a native woman. My yellow hair flared against the dark windows like a meteor. Philip removed his jacket, vest and pocket watch and joined me in the dance. He paused once to remove his shirt and shoes. The drums filled us like thunder. Our long beating toes crept toward each other on the floor till they touched and I was nearly blinded by the whiteness of the soles of his feet.

During the rest of the summer, Philip and I made our plans. Because he traveled frequently to Africa, I would live there and confer with his wife, J'tumba, only by mail. I would finish my dissertation under the best possible circumstances.

One day I got a wire from Davy that the frozen salmon was coming in at the airport and that I would have to get some dry ice before I claimed it. He advised me to borrow a pickup truck from one of the men in the Wild Game Bird Association. When I called the man, I asked him if he could locate a pair of Cleopatra birds for me. I could pay cash, I said, or if the owner preferred I could trade the birds for salmon. He put me in touch with a breeder and we settled the details.

I kept Phyllis locked in the yard with the ducks and the cats and the Valley quail and the doves and the finches till the very day Davy was due home. The salmon were all lined up in frozen rows in the freezer like stiff gray soldiers. I avoided looking at their dull silvery black eyes. I wrote Davy a note explaining that I had found funds to travel and study in Africa and that eventually he would enjoy his freedom, and could go elk hunting in Washington in the fall and not have to worry about me being home alone. I assured him he would make friends easily, and thanked him for the life we had had together and told him to be sure and look in the bedroom for a surprise.

The Cleopatra birds were waiting for him in a big silver cage with clean straw under their feet. Their tails whisked in circles over the straw as they spun round and round like two lunatics in fear of Phyllis. She was frenzied, having just been let back into the house. Saliva dripped from her chops. She circled the cage, showing teeth of yellow ivory. Her red eyes held to the birds' black eyes like magnets. I instructed her not to attack them, and for emphasis I put on her shock collar and shocked her once, head over heels, to teach her a lesson. When I saw that she had come to safely, I told her that she was to guard them carefully for Davy, her master, who would soon be home. Light-footed, I danced from the house, throwing for good measure a handful of bullet-shaped pellets to the ducks on my way out.

# We Know That Your Hearts Are Heavy

PIGEONS ARE CROWDING THE WINDOW SILL to keep out of the rain. The drizzle has just turned to downpour, and the birds have flown up from Boston Common. They are stepping on each other's toes to find a footing on the two-inch ledge. The victims of misstep do not fall six stories and spatter their blood on the pavement; they merely hang in midair, flutter a hundred wet black feathers, and immediately land back on the ledge, dancing a wild two-step to get dry.

The phone rings, and I spin around. Before I quite realize it is the phone and not my employer coming in the door, I have hidden in my lap certain papers from the top of my desk that are obviously not the work I am supposed to be doing, and have picked up a pencil, which I poise professionally over nothing. I compose myself enough to lift the receiver.

"One moment, please," says the operator, and then I hear my mother's voice coming to me from Miami.

"Mother!" I cry.

"Janet, darling, how are you?"

"Is anything the matter?"

Long-distance calls always frighten me. My family is neither rich nor sophisticated enough to call merely to talk. There is always a reason. The last call from home came because my mother heard that a hurricane was approaching Boston, and she wanted Danny and me to move out of our rickety attic apartment in Cambridge and go to a sturdy hotel until it was over.

Since my mother does not answer me immediately, I say "Are you and Daddy all right? Is Carol all right?"

"We're fine," she says. "How are you? How's Danny?"

"We're fine," I say. "Is anything new?"

"How's the weather up there in the North Pole? I thought it's suppose to be *spring*, and the low was eighteen yesterday." My mother studies the Boston highs and lows and reports to us in every letter how much better off we'd be in Miami. She cannot understand why the University of Miami would not be just as good a place for Danny to do his graduate work as Harvard.

"We had a hailstorm last night," I add, for no sensible reason.

"And how is your job?"

"It's fine, it's fine."

I wait, and then it comes. "Janet, Daddy is flying to New York this afternoon. Uncle Benny has had a heart attack."

"Oh, no," I say. "Poor Celia."

Celia is my cousin who is four days younger than I am, and who looks like Elizabeth Taylor. She is due to have her baby any day. I say this to my mother.

"She's due *today*," my mother says. "The poor child."

"Is it very serious?"

"He died, darling. Uncle Benny died."

I am silent for a moment, digesting this. My Uncle Benny is my father's elder brother. He looks just like my father (though I in no way resemble Elizabeth Taylor), and he is very rich and lives on Park Avenue in Manhattan. He has always been my favorite uncle, even though most of the relatives do not like him because of all of his money. I think he has always loved me because I look so much like him.

"How is Daddy taking it?" I say. Outside, the pigeons are now standing on each other's heads.

While my mother is saying that he is as all right as can be expected, it occurs to me that I will go to New York to see my father, whom I have not seen in a year. I tell my mother that, and she says she doesn't want me to go, and I say I will, and she puts my father on to argue with me, and suddenly I say something frightful. I tell my father that I want to come because I have never been to a funeral and I want to see what one is like.

He is angry, I am sure. I see him thinking, Do you imagine a funeral is a *show*? And I am thinking, in self-defense, It was very unfair of all of you to conceal Grandma's death from me when I was in college and not tell me till after the funeral, so that I still can't believe she is dead because I was not *there*. I have never seen anyone dead, and I am twenty-two, and I think I must not grow one day older till I do.

But my father is too preoccupied to get angry. He simply says there is nothing much to see at a funeral; he is going to fly back to Miami as soon as it is over, and in just two months, in June, he and Mother and Carol will all drive up to Boston to see us, and there's no need for me to go to any funeral, especially if the weather is bad. He does not sound very convincing or stern, though, which is strange, because those are the things my father usually is.

Finally, I say what one of us always says on long-distance calls, "This is costing a fortune," and my mother gets back on the line to tell me to keep warm, and then I remember that my Aunt Beth, Celia's mother, died less than a year ago, and I ask my mother if Uncle Benny might not have died of just being sad.

"On Park Avenue," my mother says, "a heart attack and too many sleeping pills can be the same thing," and the call is over and I am left with all kinds of terrible thoughts.

I lean forward to stare out over the Common, and the papers in my lap slide to the floor. I pick them up and set them back on the desk. They are greeting-card verses. Some-one has told me that you can sell greeting-card verse for two dollars a line. If I can sell one eight-line verse a day, I will be able to quit this job, which I hate, and stay at home and not have to go on the hideous subway every day. The money from the verses will help put Danny through graduate school just as surely as the money from this job in the publishing house.

Today I have been doing Bereavements. In the last week, I have written a number of Birthdays, Get Wells, Mother's Days, Wedding Days, Baby Arrivals, and Valentines. Today, a gloomy April day, seemed appropriate for Bereavements. I think of Uncle Benny, and then I read the verse I composed this very morning:

> We know that your hearts are heavy
> And your sorrow is very deep,
> But remember: The Lord loves all his lambs
> Who rest in Eternal Sleep.

Obviously, it is not quite right. It is not, as my title says, "A Comforting Thought During Your Time of Bereavement." But then, I have never been bereaved; it is no wonder I cannot write sincere Bereavement verses.

I decide I am going to New York despite my parents' wishes. And right now I am getting out of this office; I can't stand it here anymore. I put my verses into my purse and go down the hall to tell Mr. Cowper that I have to go to New York to a funeral, and I say it so fast and sadly that he perhaps thinks it is my father and not my uncle who has died.

I take the subway to Harvard Square and walk home from there. Danny has the hi-fi on; he is playing the sad songs of Schubert again—the rain has affected him, too—and when I get to the top of the third flight of stairs I knock on our door. He opens it and I say without looking into his eyes, "I have to go to New York to see my father. My Uncle Benny just died, and my father is flying to New York this afternoon."

"What?" says Danny, and to my horror I find myself smiling as I repeat the words.

Danny does not see. He helps me peel off my raincoat, and throws it across the back of a chair. He turns off the phonograph, and then closes the book he has been reading.

"I have to call the bus station and see when a bus leaves," I say, and at the same instant Danny is saying, "It's a bad day for such a long trip, but I think we can make it O.K. if we drive slowly."

I am shocked. It had not occurred to me that Danny will come. I have been imagining this as a private family affair. Danny does not like families, and he will not like mine. None of them are the kind of people we would have for friends, but I feel for them something akin to love, which makes them bearable, while Danny has no reason at all (except that I am his wife) to be tolerant of their crudities and illiteracies. I fear that he will be impatient, then offended, then angry, and finally will insist that I leave with him, which I will not want to do. I shall see this through to the end, even if it means disregarding Danny's wishes.

However, none of this can be explained. Danny is already saying he will have to miss his advanced seminar, but it is more important that I go to New York.

In less than twenty minutes, we are ready. We leave the attic in a mess—the bed unmade, crumbs under the kitchen table. By one o'clock, we are on the Massachusetts Turnpike. At the Connecticut state line, the rain turns into snow, and we now have to go thirty miles an hour instead of forty.

Before I understand that something has happened, Danny has stopped the car suddenly and is pulling out his wallet. In a moment, a highway patrolman is looking in my window.

"Open it!" Danny says, nearly shouting at me.

The patrolman takes Danny's license and reads it. "Are you going to a fire?" he says.

I wait for Danny to say we are going to a funeral. He says nothing. It seems he has changed lanes unsafely. The patrolman talks across me. He is very young; wet snow is clinging to his hat and to the tip of his nose. He is lecturing Danny about reckless driving, and I keep wanting to say, Please don't yell at us—it is snowing so hard, and my Uncle Benny is dead, and my father has to come thirteen hundred miles in an airplane this afternoon to see his dead brother, and my cousin has a baby in her, which is about to be born any minute.

The patrolman is now writing out a ticket, and is asking Danny if he is a student. He talks on and on, and I could kill Danny for not telling him. I want to tell everyone that someone has died whom I love. It is so important—how can anyone give us a *ticket*?

Finally, we are driving again, very slowly. Danny is chastened. His lips are tightly closed, he is trembling slightly, and I do not say anything.

We get into New York at eight-thirty, and, by calling several relatives, we learn the whereabouts of my father. He is at the Lakeview Chapel, where Uncle Benny is laid out. It takes

Danny nearly another hour to find the chapel. Though we were both born in Brooklyn, neither of us knows Manhattan. I walk a few feet in front of Danny as we approach the funeral parlor. My heart is beating very fast. In the lobby, which is very much like a hotel lobby, a man at a desk asks us which "party" we are with. "We are with the Goldman party," I say, and Danny and I look at each other.

Danny has met my Uncle Benny once, just after the death of Aunt Beth. On our honeymoon, we stopped in New York and had dinner with him. His two children were there—Celia and Fred—and Celia's husband, Glen, and Fred's wife, Melissa. Melissa was obviously pregnant, and Celia was also pregnant, though we did not know it. My Aunt Beth had always had a delicate heart, and the relatives attributed her death mainly to the fact that Melissa was a Catholic.

The night we visited, my Uncle Benny spoke very softly and sadly. He said he was getting along—he was trying to keep busy, the children came to dinner once a week, he would get used to being alone in time. After dinner, he took us aside and said, "Look, children, if you ever need anything—money, anything—you know it's here waiting for you. Just call me collect. Please remember that. You know you don't have to be bashful with me." He put one arm around me and one hand on Danny's shoulder. "You never have to worry as long as I can help you out."

Danny thanked him, and I kissed him, and for a minute he covered his eyes with his hand. Then Fred came in to show us his wedding pictures. Fred's wedding had been an immense affair, at which it was said my Uncle Benny got drunk and cried, and in nearly every picture was my Aunt Beth—a large woman, with a lovely straight nose and her hair pulled back in a chignon. None of Uncle Benny's brothers or sisters had been invited to the wedding. Only his Park Avenue friends had that honor. The youngest of the three brothers, my Uncle Sol, had said, "Benny didn't want his poor relatives from Brooklyn there. God will punish him for such a sin."

The punishment having now been visited upon Uncle Benny, Danny and I walk across the soft, deep carpet of the lobby to the elevator, and are taken to the fourth floor. There is a great commotion coming from the end of the hall. We advance, and enter an anteroom where there is a coat rack. I glance through an open door into a larger room and get the impression that everyone is standing there holding a highball. For one instant, I see my father—tall, beloved, hunched over slightly, his arms crossed over his chest as though he is cold—talking to some person I do not know. I look away, pretending I have not seen him, and Danny takes my coat and hangs it up. I stand there, looking down at my shoes, and suddenly my father is hugging me, his suit jacket scratching my cheek. I kiss him, and turn my face away, feeling tears rise and then subside. Then I look at him and say, "Oh Daddy." He hugs me again, and, remembering, releases me and shakes Danny's hand. Danny is already uncomfortable, but there is nothing I can do. I must think about other things right now. I forget about Danny, and later see him sitting alone in a corner at the far end of the room, his chin in his hand, his eyes staring at nothing.

My father, holding me tightly by the hand, does not reprimand me for coming. I understand that he is glad. We weave around groups of standing people; no one, of course, is holding a high ball, but that impression is still with me. I see the faces of aunts, uncles, cousins—all of them from the same neighborhood in Brooklyn, all of them together for the first time in probably thirty years. Most of them have not seen me since I was "so high." A few stop us to tell me that, and to marvel at the fact that I am now married. "Where is the husband?" they say, and I point to Danny, in the corner, who looks as though he might be Uncle Benny's son, the way he is sitting so quietly, staring so sadly at the rug. "Imagine!" they say. "*Married*!" Mostly, they are marveling at how old they have grown. An occasion such as this moves them to philosophy. There is talk of dying everywhere. After all, Uncle Benny was only fifty-four—it could happen to anyone.

My Aunt Ida comes over to us. She is a widow. My Uncle Benny has been supporting her and her nine-year-old daughter Charlotte for the past six years. "Janet dear," she says, "what a stunning suit you are wearing!"

I stare at her. Her brother is dead, and she is telling me I am wearing a stunning suit. Suddenly I am struck by a horrible thought—this is *Celia's* suit I am wearing! Over the years since Celia and I were children, my Aunt Beth used to make up a package of Celia's outgrown clothes every few months and send them to my mother for me. The last package had been sent about a year ago. It contained the suit I am wearing. Fred's clothes went to my Uncle Sol's son Bill. Even though both my father and my Uncle Sol now lived in Miami, my Aunt Beth, I am sure, had continued to think of them as the poor Brooklyn relatives.

In a moment, my Aunt Ida wanders off, and my father leads me firmly down the length of the room. He says softly, "Have you seen Uncle Ben?"

"No," I say. "Where is he?" at the same moment understanding that he is right in this room with us.

My father puts both hands on my shoulders and gently turns me around, and there, in front of me, is the dead man.

What, when I first came into the room, I thought was a display of flowers is not merely that. Sunk deep into hundreds of expensive blooms is a beautiful coffin. The upper half is open; the lower half is closed and covered with roses. In it lies my Uncle Ben in a navy-blue suit. He is wearing a tie. In his pocket is a handkerchief with the initials "B. G." I cannot look at his face. There is a feeling in my body I have never had before, of something stopping or freezing. My father is beside me, but I know that when I look at the face of the dead man I will see the face of my father—it does not matter that *now* it is my Uncle Ben. I look at the face. It is not my father. It is not my uncle. It is the face of someone who is not there. There are my uncle's cheeks, and his nose, which is shaped exactly like my nose, and his lips, but the color of life is gone. The feeling I have is as real as my heartbeat: he has gone out.

*But where has he gone?* I become hysterical and turn to my father.

My father steadies me, and leads me out into the hall. Near the elevator, where it is quiet, he sets me down on a bench. "Janet," he says.

I cannot control myself; it is more terrible than I can stand. My father's dear flesh, which I am touching, cannot stay forever. My mother cannot stay, Danny cannot stay, my sister Carol cannot stay. I cannot stay! It is too much to explain. I am able only to cry against me father's sleeve. Danny, who has come out after us, is holding one of my hands, and I kiss his fingers, and I kiss my father's sleeve, and then I take a deep breath and stand up.

In a few minutes, we all go back to the filled room. People are looking at me. They are probably thinking, Why is *she* so upset? It is not *her* father.

I speak to no one, and find myself, finally, beside Celia. She is in a low chair, dressed in a black maternity dress, her belly swollen so large it does not seem part of her. She is pale, but she is wearing lipstick, and her hair is fashionably combed. I feel as though she is twenty years my elder. In one year's time, she has had two deaths and a conception happen to her. Nothing has ever happened to me. I don't know what to say.

Celia says, "I'm so happy for you. It must be wonderful to see your father."

"Oh, no!" I say, but she is going on.

"It is *so* nice you could see him after so long. I'm glad someone is getting some pleasure from this."

She means to be polite—she is showing her good breeding—but what can she mean? Her finishing school has not taught her that you do not have to offer your father's life in politeness.

I say, "I'm very sorry, Celia," and she smiles at me. She is very beautiful.

Then I leave her and go to the corner in which Danny has been sitting all evening. He and I sit there together, and I watch my father go back to the coffin and stand before it with his head bowed. What is he thinking? What is he remembering? What is he feeling? "Danny," I say, "I can't stand it. I can't *under*stand it."

"Sh-h-h," he says, squeezing my hand, and that is all the help he can give me.

Just then, a little gray-haired man comes into the room. He shakes slightly from a palsy, and he makes an announcement. "Will the immediate family of the deceased view the body once again if they wish to, as the coffin must be closed in a half hour and cannot be opened tomorrow before the funeral."

He leaves as quickly as he has come, and my father moves away, to give Celia and Fred the last half hour.

Fred walks toward the coffin and looks into it, and then walks away, squeezing his eyes shut as though he has a pain in his head that he cannot endure. Celia and her husband approach it, holding hands, and stand before it for a long time. Celia's arm is now around her husband's waist, and I see her clench her hand into a fist and bang it against the small of his back in a tiny futile gesture. I am ashamed of my outburst. She is a braver person than I am.

The little palsied man comes back into the room, and Celia and Glen back away from the coffin. She does not see, but from where I am *I* see the little man take a comb out of his breast pocket, lean into the coffin, and comb my Uncle Ben's hair neatly back off his forehead. Then he lowers the top half of the coffin and seals my Uncle Ben inside.

People are getting their coats. There is some difficulty about where Danny and I will spend the night. My father is staying with my Aunt Pearl and Uncle Carl in Brooklyn. My Uncle Sol, who has flown from Miami with my father, and my Aunt Ida, who lives all the way out on Long Beach, are also staying with them. My Aunt Pearl and Uncle Carl say *we* should come home with them, too, but I know they live in a one-bedroom apartment and have no place to sleep so many people. They will manage, they say, but Danny is doubtful. He would rather we stayed at a hotel. I cannot explain to him that we *can't* stay at a hotel—this is not a night one leaves the family. He should not have come along if he cannot do what has to be done.

Fred comes up and says why don't we stay in Uncle Ben's apartment. There are three large bedrooms (he means we do not have to sleep in the bed that Uncle Ben died in); no one is using them.

Danny is willing, but my father wants me with him. He feels what I am feeling. "I haven't seen her in a year," he explains to Fred. "We'll manage somehow."

Danny and my father and I all get into our car, and we follow my Uncle Carl's car back to Brooklyn. Everyone will meet at the synagogue the next morning at eleven.

Seven people are to sleep in an apartment that has only two single beds—Danny and I, my father, my Uncle Sol, my Aunt Ida, and my Aunt Pearl and Uncle Carl. My Aunt Pearl is trying to arrange things. It seems it is a very delicate question, the delicacy lying in the fact that Danny and I are newlyweds. We are to sleep together, and yet we cannot be given a room to ourselves. Do older people think that newlyweds make love even on the eves of funerals? From their whispering and arguing, it seems so. The conclusion is that we will have to take the consequences of this death. So Danny and I are assigned one of the single beds, my Aunt Pearl and Aunt Ida, who are sisters, the other, and a beach chair is set up at the foot of our bed for my Uncle Carl to sleep on. In the living room, my Uncle Sol will sleep on the couch and my father on another beach chair.

Danny is hating this—he will not sleep in a room filled with strangers; he will not be subject to their curious opinions on young love; he will not be the object of ridiculous imaginings— but he says nothing, because he is afraid to upset me further, and I am grateful.

It is bedtime. To be done with it, Danny undresses and is the first in bed. I am next. We both feign immediate sleep. It is frightfully hot. I am wearing a high-necked flannel night-gown, packed because it was so cold in Boston when we left. It must be ninety-five degrees in the apartment. My Aunt Ida crawls into the second twin bed, which is less than a foot from our bed. She sighs. She says, to no one in particular, "Isn't it wonderful how fast the young can fall asleep?" My Uncle

Carl, who weighs over two hundred pounds, gingerly lets himself down on the beach chair, which creaks terrifyingly. "Oh God," he says.

My Aunt Ida's head is toward me, and she is breathing in my face. I am choking. I cannot move, because I am supposed to be asleep. Danny seems actually to be sleeping. It is the only sensible way out of this ridiculous situation.

For a while, there is nothing but creaks and sighs. I imagine my Uncle Sol and my father already asleep in the living room. The conferences about the sleeping arrangements have embarrassed my father, too—we did not even say goodnight. My Aunt Pearl comes into the dark room and sits down on the edge of the bed in which Aunt Ida is sleeping. Suddenly a flashlight beam illuminates the ceiling.

"For God's sake, Pearl, what are you doing?" says Uncle Carl from his beach chair.

"Sh-h-h," she says. "Setting my hair."

On the ceiling I can see the giant corkscrew of a ringlet.

"Aw, come on," Uncle Carl says. "Go to sleep, Pearl. It's nearly three o'clock."

"Shut up," she whispers. "I'll look enough like a witch already from crying." There is the clink of bobby pins. "*How* could Benny have killed himself?" she says into the dark.

"Who says that?" says Uncle Carl. "The maid found him dead in bed. A heart attack."

"Don't tell me," says Aunt Pearl. "He was living death all the time since Beth died. His heart was broken. He was a broken man."

"With all his millions?"

"Oh, shut up. Money isn't everything."

"You'll wake the children."

"They're not such children. They're married to each other."

I see on the ceiling a giant corkscrew subdued to a circle. The flashlight must be in her lap, shining up through her hair.

"I once told him to drop dead," my Aunt Pearl says. "God forgive me. I was eighteen and I wanted to go to the roller-skating rink at the Greek's. My father was dead already, and Benny was the head of the family. He said I couldn't go—it was a cheap place; he didn't want me picking up boys. I said too bad, I'm going anyway, so he grabbed me and put me over his knee and spanked me. I told him to drop dead. Heaven helped me, Carl—he's dead."

"Yeah, thirty years later," says Uncle Carl. "Look, Pearl, go to sleep. Don't make yourself suffer."

"Suffer, suffer," my Aunt Pearl says. "To be alive is to suffer." She is crying now. The beach chair creaks, and Uncle Carl's head looms on the ceiling. Then the flashlight is shut off.

"Carly, Carly," Aunt Pearl is whispering. "We should only go together. God should be good to us. I don't want to be without you—we should go at the same time."

Uncle Carl is whispering and Aunt Pearl is crying, and, finally, gratefully, I fall asleep.

I wake, and the night is not yet over. There is the sound of breathing all around me. From the living room comes the grating sound of someone snoring. Could it be my father? When I lived at home, he did not snore. But that was years ago, before I went away to college. Danny's knee is in my back and I cannot change position without falling out of bed. I hold back the blanket and step onto the floor. I tiptoe into the bathroom, where I wash my stinging eyes with cold water and comb my hair with someone's green comb. I do not know what to do. I cannot return to the narrow, stifling bed, but neither can I leave Danny there alone. What would happen if he should wake and find himself alone in the midst of all my breathing relatives?

But I will only be gone a little while. In the living room, my father is pressed into a narrow beach chair. He is snoring. I stand above him, wanting to kiss him. "Daddy," I whisper, but he does not waken.

Finally, I put my coat on over my nightgown and go outside. It is windy and cloudy, but there is a faint suggestion of dawn. My Uncle Carl's apartment is only two blocks from the house in which I spent my childhood, and I walk there. Perhaps *it* will tell me something about where the years go.

The house is smaller and meaner and uglier than I ever imagined. The front yard, which had been like a hundred acres to me, is not more than fifteen feet long. I feel cold and foolish; my nightgown is sticking out from under my coat. I go back and crawl into bed with Danny. I am grateful for his warm body, because I am shivering. The next time I wake up, it is morning.

In the living room, they are finally talking about what they have all been thinking of: the will. Uncle Sol says solemnly, "Ida, I hope you have been provided for."

Aunt Ida says, a little shortly, "There is nothing to worry about."

Uncle Ben has been supporting her for six years, and she evidently does not wish to discuss it. She sits on the couch between Uncle Sol and my father, and ruffles her short black hair with her fingers. She does not wash her hair more than once a month. She vacuums it. She uses a drapery attachment from her old Electrolux, believing that it stimulates the brain. Aunt Ida has been very superstitious since the night Uncle George died; he had a convulsive seizure on the night of a full moon, and Aunt Ida believes he was under a spell. She swears he bared his teeth at her, like a wolf, before he passed out of this life. He was not "lost" to her, though, since she felt his life force pass into her body, and she believes she has the strength to live and raise her child alone because she has two life forces bouncing about within her. For the last few years, she has been a health faddist. In her purse, she carries a dozen pill bottles.

Presently, Uncle Sol says, "We are not worried, Ida—we only hope Ben had the foresight to make a will." The brothers of the Goldman family have always looked with suspicion on wills and insurance policies. They seem like asking for trouble. "A man like Ben," says Uncle Sol, reflecting rather desperately, "a man with such a business mind must have had the foresight." Uncle Sol leans back, a frown on his forehead. It is known that Uncle Ben, in order to avoid certain income taxes, years ago put one of his corporations in Uncle Sol's name. As a return for this favor, Uncle Ben has been paying Uncle Sol's income tax every year, in addition to paying him a token salary of fifty-five dollars a week. Uncle Ben promised Uncle Sol's son, my cousin Bill, a new car on his eighteenth birthday. Bill is now seventeen. Uncle Sol's meager earnings from his fabric store will never afford Bill a new car. Neither will those earnings support Uncle Sol's family if the store is his only income. Uncle Sol sighs. "Ach," he says, "an ugly business."

"I wonder," says fat Uncle Carl, sitting on the edge of the beach chair my father slept in, "whether there was fancy paper business—accountants and lawyers, things like that."

"Sure there was," says Aunt Pearl. "A man like Ben doesn't keep his money in a piggy bank."

"I was just thinking maybe he arranged with his lawyer or someone that Ida should be taken care of if anything happened."

"There's nothing to worry about," says Aunt Ida.

Aunt Pearl says, "Carl, run out and get something for breakfast. Bagels and lox."

Carl rises. My father goes to him and presses a bill into his hand. "Buy it with this," he says.

"Don't be a big shot," Uncle Carl says, shoving it back. "I got plenty of money."

Uncle Carl has not got plenty of money. Five years ago, he sent Aunt Pearl to her brother to ask for a loan. Uncle Ben loaned them five thousand dollars to start a dry-cleaning store with. The store failed. Uncle Carl now works as a cutter in a dress factory. It is clear that Uncle Carl is wondering if Uncle Ben tore up that IOU, or if accountants will unearth it and force payment from him. He leaves to get the bagels and lox.

"What about you, Abram?" says Uncle Sol.

"*What* about me?" says my father.

"What do you think about a will?"

"I think we shouldn't worry about it. There are other things to think about this morning."

Uncle Sol is silenced. He and my father look down at their laps.

Aunt Pearl goes into the kitchen to prepare for breakfast. In a minute, she calls, "Ida, come help me."

Aunt Ida sighs, gets up from the couch, and goes into the kitchen. In a few minutes, Uncle Carl comes back with two brown paper bags. He sets them in the kitchen, and puts up two card tables in the living room. Aunt Ida returns from the kitchen, carrying one empty plate. She places it in the center of one of the card tables, and sits back down on the couch between her brothers.

We hear a cry from the kitchen. "Damn her, damn her, damn her!" Aunt Pearl is sobbing.

Carl runs to the kitchen. "Pearl! What's the matter?"

"My God-damned sister," she sobs, coming to lean against the wall of the living room and point at Ida. "I ask her to help and she carries in one lousy dish. I'm up all night, and I have to cook for everyone, and my husband sleeps on a beach chair in his own house, and she sits on her fat behind."

"Pearl," my father says, getting up and going to her. "There's no need to fight like this today. Everyone is upset. Try to calm down."

"Oh, shut up!" she screams. "Who do you think you are—big brother Ben, bossing me all over the place?"

"Stop that," my father says. "*Stop that!*"

"Just like old times," Aunt Pearl goes on, wildly. "Ida gets away with everything and I get stuck with the dirty work. Where was Ida when Mama died? Do you know where she was? She was at a *party*! That's where devoted Ida was."

"Pearl, Pearl!" cries Uncle Sol. "What's the *sense*?"

Aunt Ida is still sitting on the couch, twisting her fingers together.

"Don't *you* talk!" Aunt Pearl shouts at him. "Who do you think it was who almost *killed* Mama? *You* with that *shiksa* you nearly married!"

"ENOUGH!" My father, now the eldest brother, now the head of the family, gives the sternest order I have ever heard. "THERE WILL BE NO MORE OF THIS."

Everyone is silent.

Finally, Uncle Carl says, "Come on. Let's have breakfast."

Little by little, the air calms; we all settle down at the table. Danny has come in from the bedroom, all dressed and shaven. He looks embarrassed because he has heard the fighting. "Good morning," he says.

Aunt Ida smiles at him. She is in the midst of lining up her dozen pill bottles on the table. She offers pills to each. "Sol?

Abram? Carl? Janet?" We shake our heads. She says softly, "Pearl, you?" Another no. Then, hesitantly, "Danny?"

Danny accepts. Aunt Ida beams. Into his palm she pours pills of many colors, shapes, contents. This is for good blood, this is for the circulation, this is for the liver. One is more mysterious—it is for life force. Danny doesn't wince. He swallows them seriously, one by one. Aunt Ida loves him. She smiles at my father—Your daughter has married a fine boy. She smiles at me—You have a fine husband. Everyone feels a little better.

On the table are onion rolls, bagels, rye bread. There is butter and cream cheese. There is whitefish and lox and sour cream and bananas and pickled herring. There is coffee and cream and sugar.

Everyone begins to talk about what a good man Ben has always been. It cannot be denied that he has been very generous to all of them. If he did not mingle with them socially, it has to be understood. After all, his friends were a different type; Beth was a different type. But Ben never forgot his family. They were never in need. Ben always believed blood ties were the strongest ties on earth.

Uncle Sol bursts out, "But why should *he* have been the only one to go to college? Why did the rest of us have to work in the clothing factory? Why was *he* the only one who was Bar-Mitzvahed? It wasn't fair." He seems close to tears.

Now they are bringing up old grievances. Ben had everything; they had nothing. Ben had an education, Ben had a car, Ben had a *chance*. They had no chance. They are all failures.

My father nods. He is agreeing that he is a failure. It is not possible for me to stand in front of all these people and tell him he is not a failure. I love him. He has done everything for me and for Mother and for Carol. He has worked like a dog in fifteen different businesses and sent me through college; he will send Carol through college. He has taught us to think, he has given us strength to cope with pain and fear, he has taught us to be honest and fair.

Aunt Pearl, who has been silent since the fight, now says, "It's ironical. Don't envy. He's dead, this brother of ours who had everything. His Beth is dead, his children are orphans, his grandchildren he will never see. Such good fortune, such luck is that?"

They are silent, considering. Indeed, the tables have been turned. Here they all sit in Brooklyn, eating bagels and lox, while Ben is in a coffin on his way to the synagogue.

"May he rest in peace," my father says. "No more talk now."

They observe that it is late, it is time to get started. The service is being held at eleven. The table is cleared quietly.

My father tells me to wear something warm. It is windy and rainy again, the worst kind of day for putting away in the earth. Again something is stopping, freezing in me.

We drive through Brooklyn, through Prospect Park, through downtown, across the East River into Manhattan. Somewhere, on the busiest parkway, we have a flat tire. We *can't* have one; we are already late. "Don't worry," says Uncle Carl. "They can't go ahead without us. They will wait." He must be thinking, but not saying, that Benny will wait, too.

My father is out of the car, kneeling on the road. His face is red with the strain of taking off the tire. "Danny!" I cry. "Help him!" He is only two years younger than Uncle Benny.

The flat tire is fixed; we go on. We are aware of how risky the world is.

At the synagogue, I feel dizzy and weak from lack of sleep. Downstairs is a ladies' room. My Aunt Pearl is there before me; she is powdering under her eyes. "Janet," she says to me, "life is worse than you know," and she is gone. I stay there and try to quiet my stomach. I am afraid for my father. I have never seen him cry, but I am afraid I will see him cry today.

When I come up the stairs, an attendant stops me and says I am too late—I will have to wait outside.

"Wait outside?" I cry.

"Are you related to the deceased?" he asks.

"I am his niece," I say, and push past him. I am at least as important to this service as the Wall Street cronies who are here. They cannot keep me out. My father is waiting for me.

All the relatives are in a long line at the back of the room. The front three rows of seats are empty; the rest of the temple is filled. This is the Park Avenue congregation. These are all Uncle Benny's rich friends. We walk down the aisle. My father is holding my arm as he did at my wedding. Danny is walking behind us, alone. The line files into the front row. My father takes the last seat, and there is no room for me next to him. I have to sit in the second row, diagonally behind him.

Celia is also in the front row, looking as though she has not slept at all. She is wearing a black hat with a thin veil that covers her eyes.

The rabbi begins to speak. With a shock I see the coffin, not two feet from my father, right under the platform on which the rabbi stands. The top is completely covered with roses. It is so magnificent a box you can almost see the congregation reflected in its polished sides.

The rabbi is saying what a good man Uncle Ben was, that all of us know what an honor it is for a man's remains to be brought under the sacred roof of the shul. This good man was president of the Men's Club. No matter how busy he was, he never missed a Friday-night service. He was religious and pious and honorable. Sometimes, on a weekday morning, he would come into the temple alone and sit at the back, staring at the Ark of the Covenant. Ben Goldman was a fine man. Ben Goldman loved all his children.

When he says that, he looks at the front row, where Melissa sits next to Fred, and he repeats, "He loved *all* his children." The Catholic daughter-in-law is included. This is a generous rabbi.

What the rabbi cannot mention—and what perhaps is Uncle Ben's greatest achievement—is that Uncle Ben has just been given a larger writeup in a new book called *Moneymakers* than anyone else in the country has been given. He has been described as the shrewdest chemical man in America in this book. A photograph shows him watching a ticker tape, a far from pious expression on his face.

The rabbi says, "And now this good soul has gone to join his beloved Beth," and I see my father cover his eyes, and I begin to cry. Danny takes my hand, but I gather momentum and am shaking so hard I cannot breathe.

Men come forward and lift the coffin. Very slowly, they walk toward the back of the shul, rose petals slipping off the coffin to fall under their feet. My father is the first to follow the coffin out. I drop Danny's arm and run ahead to hold my father's. He averts his face, and from deep in his chest I hear a ripping sound that I know is the sound of a man crying who had not cried in forty years.

Outside, in the wind, he is in control again. There are seven black limousines lined up to take the mourners to the cemetery. My father opens the door of the third limousine. "Get inside. I don't want you to catch cold."

"Where are you going?"

He points to the second car.

"I want to go with you," I say.

"I have to go with the brothers and sisters."

He won't let me argue. I get into the third limousine. In the second are the brothers and sisters, in the first the children of Ben and their mates, and in front of that the hearse, with Uncle Ben under his roses.

Danny leans back uncomfortably in one of the seats that have been pulled up from the floor—the most uncomfortable in the car. There are six strangers with us in the car. The driver is a pock-marked, yellow-skinned, unpleasant-looking man. Beside him are a couple with bored faces. In back of us are two middle-aged women and one very old woman.

The car moves slowly away from the curb. It is daytime, but the headlights of the cars in the procession are on. The yellow-faced driver maneuvers skillfully in the heavy traffic. This is just another working day for him.

One of the middle-aged women leans forward and taps me on the shoulder. "Are you related to Benny?" she asks in a rasping, masculine voice.

"His niece," I say.

"Are you Abie's girl?"

"Yes."

"I thought so. You look like him, I lived next door to your father in Bensonhurst. I was his first girl. My name is Mickey."

I am repelled. My father has as much as betrayed my mother with this vulgar woman.

"I didn't use to talk this way," she explains. "I had part of my voice box removed. Cancer."

The little old lady now taps me on the shoulder. "You want I should show you the pictures of my grandchildren? I'm your father's Aunt Sadie."

So this is Aunt Sadie, the aunt my father dislikes most. I do not know why, exactly, but I do know her husband owned a clothing warehouse and gave my father—then a boy of eleven—the night watchman's job in it. My father used to sit shivering in the dark, hearing rats run across the floor and imagining horrors he can hardly explain. For this he was paid twenty-five cents a night, while the same uncle sent Benny to Hebrew school.

The old lady is showing me snapshots. "This is Ruthie, she had a birthmark big as an apple, the biggest doctor in New York took it off, she's a beauty now, you could never know."

I nod wearily.

"They kicked me out from the family," she says. "Last winter, I was in Miami Beach, I called your father, he should come to see me at my hotel, he never came. Same with Sol. Probably the wives didn't let. I never liked your mother."

"Look," I say, "we're going to a funeral. Maybe we should all be a little quiet."

She sits back, silent.

We are out of the city at last. It can't be much longer. The couple in the front seat light cigarettes. The pock-marked driver then lights a cigarette for himself. We are coming into open country. The old lady taps me again. "Here," she says. She stuffs something folded into my hand. "That boy next to you must be your husband. I know you had a wedding. I was never invited, but I don't hold no grudge. Just because I was never invited is no reason I can't give a present."

It is a five-dollar bill. "Look, Aunt Sadie," I say. "I don't want it. It's not necessary."

"I have nothing against you," she says. "It's your mother who didn't invite me. Buy yourself something."

We are pulling into the cemetery. My heart pounds and I see a blackness before my eyes for an instant.

\* \* \*

The wound of my Aunt Beth's grave is not yet healed, and beside it a new one is open. They are sliding the coffin out of the hearse and carrying it toward the grave. A green rug is placed over the hole, a board across the rug, and the coffin upon the board. This is done very quickly, even before all the limousines are empty.

There is a canopy covering both graves. No tombstone marks Beth's grave; it is not yet a year. A chair is brought forward for Celia. She declines it with a shake of her head.

The canopy flaps in the wind, and the rabbi steps under it, carrying a closed black umbrella. The relatives gather in, and once again the gray-haired, palsied undertaker appears, now distributing long-stemmed red roses, one to each person. His expression is as blank as if he were dealing out a deck of cards.

I try to see past Celia's face into her thoughts. What if that were my father, locked in that coffin? What if his face were being put away from me forever? And then I ask myself a question against all knowledge. How do they know the dead are dead? What if, tonight, Uncle Ben opens his eyes and calls to be freed? Is Aunt Beth lying beneath this very earth, listening? Is she thinking, Finally, Ben, you are coming to sleep?

It seems against all things human, to bury someone under the earth who has breathed in light and air from the instant of birth. Why not lay the dead among green trees, in the open woods? Are not the ants and beetles better than the lead-sealed, waterproof, airtight, thousand-dollar mahogany casket?

My head is spinning in the pain of its own inadequacy. What does it *mean* for Uncle Benny to be dead?

The rabbi is reading the service in Hebrew. I do not understand it. At the end, at a signal of the rabbi's hand, Celia and Fred step forward. Celia steps too far, upon the unsupported part of the green rug, and lunges forward, nearly falling into the grave underneath. She is caught by my father and Fred, who hold her until she can balance herself again. Fred takes her hand, and the brother and sister say the Mourner's Kaddish: "*Yisgadal veyiskadash Sh'may rabbo be'olmo…*" They say it well—they have said it often for their mother. For a moment, I believe in the prayer; I believe there is God, this is His language, He is there, and Uncle Ben is all right. But my disbelief is suspended only until Celia steps back, nearly staggering, her face gray with anguish.

"Throw the rose," says the rabbi. Celia tosses the rose upon the coffin. Fred does the same. We all toss our roses forward, as though we are playing a game of quoits, and it is over. They are hurrying the pregnant girl out of the wind and back into the limousine.

But it is not quite over. The brothers and sisters of Uncle Ben remain behind. The four of them are crying, facing in the world's four directions, away from each other. Privately, each one is accepting the finality of his brother's death. It seems they are ashamed to look at each other, for when they are done with whatever each has had to do in his heart, they still do not draw together.

We pile back in the cars, in the same distribution as before, and we drive away.

There. I have seen a funeral—I have seen it all, and what do I know? I have understood nothing.

It is silent all the way back to Manhattan. The funeral party meets in Uncle Ben's apartment, where his maid, the colored woman who discovered his body, serves us corned-beef sandwiches and potato salad.

It is announced that the family will sit *Shiva* in two places— the brothers and sisters at Aunt Pearl's house, the children at Celia's house. But it is understood that Celia and Fred will not serve out the week of mourning, sitting on boxes on the floor, barefooted, the men unshaven, the women without color, the mirrors covered with sheets. They are of the modern generation; they have obligations; one of them has got to get a child born, the other has to learn the chemical business. Let the old folks sit *Shiva*.

Pleading his wife's tiredness, Celia's husband takes her away. Melissa and Fred leave with them. The strangers go, and the rest of us are left in Uncle Ben's house.

"There was no will," Uncle Sol says. "Fred told me." So. All the money is to go to the children. No car for Sol's son, no rent for Aunt Ida. And do even *I* feel a little disappointed?

Nothing matters. I am sick of it all. I want to go home with Danny to our rickety attic where we bang our heads on the ceiling every time we get out of bed. I want to go back to my tiny office and watch the pigeons strutting on my windowsill, which overlooks the Common. There are things to do—many things to do—and I understand that that is the only answer I shall have to all my questions.

# A Daughter of My Own

E VERY GIRL I KNOW who has ever had a baby has had her mother come and stay with her for two weeks—or her mother and a nurse—and each one tells me how wonderful it was and how she never could have survived without her mother's advice and help and soothing presence.

I just don't know. I think I love my mother as much as any girl loves hers, and I think I have always got along better with my mother, on the average, than most girls do with theirs. But if I never have another baby, it won't be because I didn't like being pregnant or being in labor or losing six months' worth of sleep; it will be because I won't know what to do about my mother.

When I found out in September that I was pregnant, and told my mother I was due to have the baby in April, she immediately began making plans to fly up "in February or March, whenever you want me." It had never occurred to me that I would want her at all. I mean, it was my baby, and we were very far away from my parents and they didn't have the money to toss away on airplane trips, and my husband was a student at the time and at home nearly all day to give me any help I might need, and there just wasn't room for anyone.

There was hardly room for the baby. Danny and I lived in a three-room apartment near the university, and had figured that by gouging out the shelves from a built-in-the-wall living room bookcase we could just manage to squeeze in a tiny crib for the baby. We hadn't exactly planned on enlarging our family just yet, and there was quite a bit of arranging to do in those early months. Not that we were unhappy about it—far from it; it just took some adjusting.

My husband was happy to adjust to a baby, but not to a mother-in-law. What bothered him most, to begin with, was that if she came before I had the baby, he would be left alone in the house with her for five days while I was in the hospital. I could see what he meant; my mother wasn't one to discuss Aristotle and Danny wasn't one to discuss the upbringing of children—at least, not with my mother and not the upbringing of *his* child.

It was hard to tell her not to come before the event, because I know what was on her mind. To put it rather simply, she wanted to hold my hand. My mother had always held my hand through crises—I had been a very sickly child, and I think that in those frightening years when doctors loomed everywhere, the grip of my mother's fingers was all that sustained me.

Now I was having a baby. People sometimes died in childbirth, I knew, and even when you made it through, it could be pretty rough. My mother had nearly died having me, and I knew how worried she was and why she wanted to be around to whisper encouragement at the hardest moments. The only difference, I felt, was that this was not a crisis. I was not sick; I was not frightened; I was not worried. I was in perfect health, I liked and trusted my doctor and I loved the little thumps I was beginning to feel down where my appendix had once been. Most important of all, though, was that I *had* someone to hold my hand if necessary—my husband.

I don't suppose my mother gave Danny much credit for being useful in any situation. After all, we had been married for three years and I had been supporting him—while all he did, as far as my mother could tell, was lounge around in unpressed pants all day reading books.

I tried to show my mother how calm and unworried I was. I sent her diagrams of the fetus in different stages of development with long, technical explanations about its growth. I recommended books on childbirth for her to read that told how simple and safe the procedure was these days. I wrote her with the gain of every new ounce, knowing she believed that gaining weight meant being healthy. I had Danny take pictures of me in different smiling poses, my jolly wave saying, "See? Nothing is wrong with *me*."

Finally I was able to persuade my mother to come right *after* the baby was born. When she agreed, though reluctant and somewhat hurt, I was able to relax and enjoy the remainder of my pregnancy. I saw every old Tarzan movie on television that had ever been made. I sat at the window on gray afternoons with all the lights off and watched the snow come down. I spent long hours staring up at the ceiling from my bed, imagining my baby and imagining me with my baby.

Danny was home nearly all that winter, studying for his comprehensives, and we talked to each other mostly at dinnertime, usually about what names we would like the baby to have and how we wouldn't do to him the bad things we thought had been done to us. It was a fine, snowy, happy winter—wet and icy outside, warm and steamy inside. I bought eight dozen diapers in my ninth month and washed them all three times by hand so they would be soft for the baby. Danny bought a used crib and we painted it and got a new mattress. We read Dr. Spock, *Childbirth Without Fear*, Gesell. We were ready.

The baby started to come on the very day he was scheduled to, which made us think that he had a most reliable character. We saw the doctor in the afternoon and he told us to go home and call him when there was "some real action." So we went home and we timed all the warming-up pains, and soon it was dark out and I was warming up a little faster. We played all six Brandenburg Concertos while I lay on the living-room couch and Danny sat on the floor next to me with his wristwatch in his lap. At eleven we called the doctor, who said, "This sounds like it. Come on down."

The snow had changed to rain, and it was a very appropriate, dramatic night for racing to the hospital. I knew, though, from the hospital brochure I had, that if we arrived before midnight we would be charged for the entire day, so I cautioned Danny to drive as slowly as he could. We meandered to the hospital— even circling a few extra blocks to kill time—until the baby made it known we had better meander no more.

We parked in the hospital lot at four minutes to midnight. I was game to sit it out till twelve, but Danny was beginning to get glassy-eyed and I was not as confident as I sounded, so we went in and signed the admittance form.

Danny was permitted to stay with me as long as I wanted to be awake, and we stayed together until nearly dawn, having a very sweet, dreamy time, holding hands, and making faces at each other every time a nurse came in to listen to the baby's heartbeat or time a contraction.

When he went away I was floated into an elevator on a very soft, high bed, and in the morning I had a little girl, six pounds, two ounces.

I truly had never felt better. It was a bright, sunny morning, and I was cranked up on my neat white bed and the light was coming in right on my knees, making them warm and comfortable. I had just seen my baby, pink and perfect, asleep, and more beautiful than any beautiful thing I had ever seen in the world.

I drifted about in the bright sunlight for a while and then Danny peeked into the room, grinning like mad, and we had a big kiss and a tremendous long smile together and then I sent him off to see his daughter.

He was with me all afternoon, but occasionally went out into the hall when a nurse came in to poke my stomach and take my pulse and temperature.

He came back one time with roses for me, and I felt like a queen there in the sunshine, all loved and loving, and I thought we had just begun to get happier than we had ever been.

When they came in with my dinner, Danny got up to leave, and I remembered that he hadn't called my mother. I told him to do that right away, and he said he would, but it seems he drove home first and had dinner and fell asleep, and it wasn't till about ten at night that he remembered to call, and the baby had been alive nearly twelve hours by then.

Everything started falling apart. My mother called me the next day at the hospital, when I could walk to the phone, and the first thing she said was, "Why didn't Danny call me right away?" So I made up something about his wanting to make sure I was all right before he called, but it wasn't very pleasant to argue and to come out of that gentle haze I'd been in, and I resisted it. I said I had to hang up and go back to bed because I was getting dizzy, but my mother managed to mention that she was coming in two days, when I would be ready to go home.

I spent the rest of the afternoon worrying about her coming and feeling very helpless and unhappy. They brought the baby to me only twice for the first two days, to get her used to me and me to her. There was no sense in her coming oftener, since she wanted mostly to sleep and my milk hadn't come in yet. It was very fine to hold her, and each time the nurse left I would undo her little kimono and examine her tiny body and count all her toes and fingers.

After they took her back to the nursery I would get worried again about my mother, and I'd feel bad till the next time they brought the baby to me. When I told Danny my mother was really coming, tears came to my eyes, and he tried to cheer me up by saying that as long as she *had* to come she would be a great help, but he didn't sound very convinced himself.

My mother arrived the evening of my fourth day in the hospital. I was to leave the next morning. Danny had a night class, so no one met her at the airport, and she took a taxi to the hospital and dragged her suitcase by herself, and when she came up to the desk they told her it was final feeding time and no more visitors were allowed until morning. She told them she hadn't seen me for a year and some kind lady let her up, and she came into my room just as the baby finished nursing. Without a word I held out the baby to her and she took her, and we both were crying, because it had been so long and we loved each other so much and now I had a daughter of my own.

But even though I was so happy to see her, that perfect moment couldn't last very long, and it didn't. Immediately she was asking if we could pay the hospital bill, since Danny was obviously not earning any money, and then asking again why Danny had waited so long to call her, and asking if I had had "too terrible a time." Nothing had seemed wrong till then, and suddenly I was worrying about the hospital bill and feeling very sorry for myself because it was hard to sit down and my breasts ached while they were getting used to the baby's nursing schedule. I didn't want to feel bad—I wanted to stay feeling like that queen in the sunshine for a while—but it was too complicated; we were talking about practical things and old rifts were coming up.

As my mother left to meet Danny downstairs and go home with him, she said, "Do you want me to come with Danny in the morning when he picks up you and the baby?" and I said, "Whatever you like," hoping she would understand that I really meant, "This is a private time and it would be nicer for the three of us to be alone."

But the next morning she was there, very proud and pleased, giving directions to everyone. "Danny you go down to the cashier, and I'll stay here and help Janet pack her things and then we'll have the nurse dress the baby." Then she asked me if I had a nursing brassiere and I said no, so she went down to the gift shop and bought me two for five dollars each, and I knew she couldn't afford it and neither could we. Everyone was bustling around so, I could hardly think of what time in my life it was—the time that I was taking my little baby home, where I would be her mother for the rest of my life.

We drove home, my mother sitting in the back seat, leaning over my shoulder all the way and looking at the sleeping baby in my lap and touching her little curled fingers and saying how beautiful she was—which was true, but somehow seemed false with my mother saying it aloud like that. Danny didn't speak all the way home, and when we got to the house he took my suitcase and went inside, and my mother and I sat in the car waiting for him to come out and open the door for me, which he didn't do. After five foolish minutes I had to open the car door myself, nearly dropping the baby and nearly crying, and my mother gave me a look that said all she had always thought of Danny. It nearly broke my heart to have everything ruined when it could have been so fine.

I went inside and put the baby in her crib, but didn't know what to do then. Danny had gone into the kitchen with a book, and was sitting at the table reading. I wanted him to admire the baby and tell me what a fine child I had produced and what a brave girl I was, but he never raised his eyes. It seemed as though I had not seen him in years, and I was missing him because I had been away from him for five days in the hospital and, in a way, all the months before than when, if he so much as gave me a kiss, my already overburdened heart would begin to shudder to remind me that warm kisses would have to wait until the baby did not demand so much blood and energy of it.

And now we were further apart than ever.

My mother took over. "You get into bed," she said. "I'll take care of the baby. You need to rest."

"But I want to look at her," I protested.

"You'll look later—you just got out of the hospital." She took off my coat and led me into the bedroom and tucked me into bed and closed the door, to leave me aching and open-eyed and missing my baby and my husband.

The baby, because she was small, had to nurse every two and a half hours and each feeding lasted nearly an hour, so I was never able to sleep for much more than an hour at a time. The nursing I had loved so much in the hospital became a terrible ordeal at home because neither Danny nor my mother could be in the room together with me and the baby at that time without becoming very embarrassed. If one was in the room and the other inadvertently came in, they both would avert their eyes, as though neither would acknowledge to the other his intimate relationship with me.

The baby and I had done beautifully in the hospital, but now, with everyone avoiding everyone in our three rooms, and doors being closed as they went in or out and me being so exhausted and tense, the baby sucked less and cried more, and made me desperate for relief of some kind—sleep, at least, or a little privacy and quiet. Privacy was what we lacked most— I wanted to be alone with my baby, I wanted to be alone with Danny and I wanted the three of us, so newly a family, to have some time alone. My mother, though, was everywhere. If Danny went over to the crib to look at the infant, my mother would appear and look too—and look at Danny to see his reaction. He would mumble and walk away.

On the third day my mother said, "I've never seen Danny kiss the baby. Doesn't he like her?"

What could I answer—"You haven't seen him kiss me either"? or: "He'd kiss her if you weren't watching all the time"? So I just sighed and asked her to bring me a drink of water. "Nursing makes me very thirsty," I told her.

That week my mother prepared all the meals and called us when they were ready. She washed the baby's diapers every day and hung them up outside. She rocked the baby so I could sleep, she cleaned the apartment from ceiling to floor, she baked my favorite chocolate cake, she fixed the hems of my skirts, she ironed, she labored like ten mules.

And it was horrible. One night in bed—my mother was sleeping on the couch in the living room—Danny whispered to me, "I'm sorry Janet, if I seem awful to her and to you, but I can't stand this. I don't feel as though this is my home anymore. I feel as though I were courting you again and calling for you at your mother's house—the way she calls us to meals and is so polite, and the way she just goes into our closets and drawers as if it were her own house. I feel as if I don't belong here."

I took his head in my arms and held him, but he said, "I really can't stand it, Janet," and then he asked me to please do some of the cooking and dishwashing so my mother would remember it was she who was visiting us and not us visiting her. "I know you're tired and still a little sick, but you have to show her what she's doing to us."

So the next day I started to wash the dishes after breakfast, though I hadn't slept three hours in twenty-four, and my mother asked me if I was crazy and told me to get back into bed that minute. I said no, I felt fine, I was getting stronger every day, and then I fainted.

Which made Danny even sadder than he had been, and soon he just left the house in the morning and went to the library and didn't come back till supper time. He had yet to hold the baby.

So I stayed in bed, and my mother brought my meals to me and brought the baby in for me to nurse and did the changing and dressing. Soon she would not even wake me if it was feeding time, but would make up a formula bottle and give it to the baby so as not to disturb me. And soon I wasn't having enough milk because the pattern was destroyed.

One night when the baby started crying, I leaped out of bed and lifted her from her crib and carried her back to my bed with me, where I was going to wake Danny and tell him to look at his daughter. But suddenly my mother was right in our bedroom, white and disheveled in her nightgown, her gray hair disordered from sleep, her arms out for the baby. "Give her to me, Janet—I'll get her quiet. You go back to sleep."

I couldn't help what I said and it was wrong of me, but I said, "Why on earth do you have to come poking around every minute? Why can't you leave us alone?"

And my mother, horrified, went right out of our bedroom. I heard her walking around in the living room all the rest of the night, while I sat in the bedroom with the baby in my lap till the sun rose.

In the morning my mother's eyes were red, she said it was because she had a cold and she was going to fly home because she didn't want the baby to catch anything from her. It was only the end of the first week, and she had planned to stay two. I knew all I had to do was ask her to please stay, and she needed me to—her eyes on my face were so pitiful—but all I did was say that I was surely much stronger now and could manage alone. Danny spoke for the first time in days, to volunteer to take her to the airport.

My mother and I couldn't look at each other—both of us had tears on our cheeks all morning—and she packed and I pretended to be busy in the bedroom.

On the way to the airport she said from the back seat, "I had to borrow on Daddy's life-insurance policy to get enough money for plane fare. I suppose I should have stayed home. You didn't need me."

"I did, oh, I *did*, Mother," I cried. And then, recognizing the lie exposed by this solemn trip, I fell silent, while my mother fumbled for a handkerchief.

"I thought you would need me," she said. The grief in her voice was so deep that I reached back for her hand, to hold it, but she pulled it away and looked out the window. "A good day for a flight," she said, making her voice steady.

My hand dropped to my lap, where my daughter lay asleep, wrapped in a blanket, and I touched her cheek, thinking: Will you and I ever come to this?

At the airport Danny wanted to go up on the observation deck because we were early, and he paid three dimes to get us through the turnstile. As soon as we got there my mother said, "It's too windy here for the baby. Let's go down." Danny said, "A little wind can't hurt her," and my mother said, "Wind is the worst thing for an infant not even two weeks old yet," and I said, "Oh, please, let's not fight—it is a warm wind, Mother," and she said, "Have it your way. I have to get on that plane."

She went down, and in about two minutes we went down too, and she had checked her luggage and was ready to leave.

"Good-bye, Mother," I said. "Thank you for coming."

She stood stiffly, looking at my face as though she didn't know me, and then she began to walk toward the gate. I ran after her and threw my arms around her and hugged her, crying, "I love you, Mother, I love you." We embraced desperately, as though this were the last time we could ever express our love, and then she went through the gate, her head down, her hand to her eyes.

I went back to Danny, who stood to one side with the baby, and shouted at him, "Why couldn't you have let her kiss the baby good-bye? Why couldn't you? Why did you have to carry her away like that?" He didn't answer me, just put the baby in my arms and then put his arm around my shoulder and began to lead me to the car. When we got outside I did not even look at the plane my mother was flying away in. We walked to the car and the wind blew the baby's cap off, and I yelled at Danny, "It *is* too windy for the baby. My mother was right! Don't you see? She was *right*!"

The cap, filling with wind, flew and bumped across the parking lot, and Danny and I watched it until it got tangled under the wheel of a car, and then we just left it there and drove home.

# Latitude

MARTHA STOOD under the bright dining-room light behind her mother-in-law, snipping deftly at the gray hairs high on the thick, slightly wrinkled neck. Funny, she thought, that she would trust me at her back with a sharp instrument. She clipped the hairs neatly, feeling them brush her legs as they fell to the floor. When she got home, she would have to shake out her shoes.

The noise in the apartment was nearly unbearable. Harry, her father-in-law, had the television turned up as loud as it would go, and above it he was singing "la-la-la" to the baby, who shrieked in delight for more. Will sat on the couch, behind the Sunday paper, doing in his head whatever he always did to avoid what went on during these visits to his parents' house.

"A little more on this side," Edna said. "It's uneven. They nearly butchered me last time. Not to say anything bad about you, but if I have to pay a fortune for an awful haircut, I'd rather let you do it." She turned toward the living room and yelled, "For God's sake, Harry, you'll frighten the baby to death with all that noise!"

"She loves it, she loves it."

"Is anyone watching the television?"

"Will is watching it. It's a documentary on Red China. It's very interesting."

"Are you watching it, Will?" Edna called, turning in the chair so that the towel around her neck came loose.

"What? No, I don't care."

"Then shut it off, Harry. No one is watching it."

"I'll get Ed Sullivan, then," he said. "Lena Horne is on."

Her mother-in-law settled back in the chair and sighed. Martha went on with her cutting.

Her poor father-in-law—he lived all week for Ed Sullivan, and then when she and Will came, he felt he had to get something intellectual on the screen for Will to watch. He probably didn't see Ed Sullivan once in ten Sundays. Who could have imagined their trooping here Sunday after Sunday for these cozy visits? Well, maybe it would do the baby some good— the Family Unit, relationships with members of the older generation, something like that.

"Bend your head, Edna. I'll get these bottom hairs and then I think we'll be done."

She could never say "Edna" without a hesitation. By right— and she knew her in-laws wished it desperately—she should call them Mother and Dad. For her own part, she'd have preferred Mr. and Mrs. Roth. But she couldn't; now that she was Mrs. Roth herself, she had to separate from the name some of the hatred for it she'd once felt. So she called them Edna and Harry, thinking each time of the names her own mother had given them in the painful days when she and Will were dating: "Hatchet Face" for Edna, and "Thunder Head" for Harry. Her mother had not done it out of spite, but to entertain Martha and make her laugh when she would come in crying after Will had related some new threat his parents had made to separate him from her.

She would never to her dying day understand the way they had acted. She'd asked herself a thousand times—not quite as much in the last few years, but still often enough—why, *how* they could have hated her so much. In her seventeenth year, when it was almost as hard for Will to get away to see her as it would have been for him to rob a bank, she'd told herself, "All right, I'm not rich, I'm not beautiful, but I'm not a whore, for God's sake, nor pregnant, nor out for his money—he hasn't any, heaven knows—and I'm from respectable people, and I'm moderately intelligent, and, genetically speaking, if Will and I have a baby, it's likely to have his brown hair and eyes, and probably his chin and nose, too, and for that matter nearly his everything, since *he* had his parents' everything," which seemed to her to prove that they dominated, body and soul, whatever they begot.

She never had even a hint of what it was they hated. Just a few days ago, she'd been cleaning out the hall closet, and she found a carton of letters she'd written to Will in the four years when they'd sent him away from her to a college in Illinois. Tucked in with her own were letters from his parents, which she had read without a qualm of conscience. Most of them said something like "Enclosed is this week's money. Please acknowledge. We've not had a letter from you in weeks." One of them read:

> Daddy and I hope you are taking advantage of your freedom to go out with other girls and see what you have been missing. We expect you will not waste your time and *our* money by writing hundreds of letters to Martha, who I'm sure is not sitting around waiting for you. Your mistake was in settling on the first thing that came along, and being as lazy as you are not making any effort to look

further for something better. Believe us when we say you would have settled for much less than the best if you'd ended up with her. She and her family were trying to trap you into something you hadn't the sense to realize. It wouldn't hurt you to write to us. NOW.

Love,<br>Mother

Martha pulled the towel off her mother-in-law's neck and shook it out. "All done," she said, and, putting the scissors on the table, she went into the living room and scooped the baby up in her arms, burying her nose in the sweet flesh of her neck, saying, "Kiss, kiss," and loving her tickled laugh, like the sound of bells rolling downhill.

She caught Will looking over his paper at her, and when their eyes met he winked, and then, embarrassed, glanced uncomfortably around the room to make sure no one had seen him. He rustled the papers loudly, and, as always happened when they were here, he receded from her into his sullen truce against his parents, determined they should have no piece of his life to conjecture upon when they were alone. But the look Martha had had from his eyes told her again that the bitter battle of wills had been worth it, and a sense of well-being flooded her body, because life was sweet now; they had their home, the baby was beautiful, they were young, and she and Will had love in their marriage.

Edna was touching the back of her hair with her short round fingers. "If I tell you I don't like it," she said, "you can always say the dinner was awful."

Martha smiled. Amazed once again at her own politeness and good manners, she thought of the day she and Will had become engaged. It was during Christmas vacation of Will's third year in college. Telling his parents proved to be an error, but Will had thought it the best strategy at the time, feeling that an outright declaration would show them he meant business, and perhaps hoping that they might by kinder. He wanted his parents to understand that he and Martha would do nothing foolish till he finished school. Just an engagement. No wedding, no babies, no having to leave college and drive a truck for a living. Just a quiet promise, and some peace. He had gotten her a ring, very thin real gold with a tiny knot of gold in the center instead of a stone—it only cost eight dollars—and they had bravely gone together into his parents' house to announce the news.

His mother had turned purple. "What right have you to ruin my son's life? Who do you think you are, trying to make a boy into a man? He's still a baby. Look at her!" she cried to her husband. "Look how she holds his hand! Look at them!"

And Will's father had become wild. "You get out of here!" He waved his fist. "You keep away from our boy!"

"What right? What right?" his mother kept shouting, and Martha, nineteen years old and pleading the only truth she knew, had said, "Because I love him," and then they were both pushing her out the door, screaming "Bitch! Bitch!" and she had fled, blind in her tears, hearing Will come down after her, shouting over his shoulder a hoarse curse at his parents.

Well, they'd survived. Witness the present scene. Spaghetti for dinner, Ed Sullivan on television, granddaughter on the rug—with Will's eyes, Will's nose, Will's chin.

"Who wants an apple?" her father-in-law said. "Will, you want an apple?"

Will, behind his papers, did not hear or did not bother to answer.

"Martha?"

"No thanks."

"Edna?"

"No, I'm going in to wash my hair. I'll be out in ten minutes."

Martha watched her mother-in-law walk through the doorway into the bedroom, her short squat form calling up none of the anguish Martha had once felt whenever she saw it. From time to time after that terrible Christmas, Martha would see his mother in a department store, or walking along the street, or coming out of a movie with her husband, and each time she'd feel faint with fear—of them, and of her murderous will toward them. She would have sworn on her life then that no change of fates would ever find her speaking humanely and decently to these people. Not even if they were to get down on their knees to her.

The funny thing was, there had been no apology at all. After years of their not speaking (her in-laws, of course, had not been at the wedding), Edna had called them one Saturday when the baby was three months old, and talked with Will. She invited him to come with the baby and Martha to dinner the next night, and Will had said Yes, and had hung up, his hand shaking.

"Why did you say Yes?" Martha had asked him. "How can we go? What do they want to do to us now?"

"I think they want to apologize," Will had said.

His parents had been terribly polite, all right, and they had nearly stood on their heads for the baby's pleasure, and they had served a good dinner—and all the while Martha's teeth were chattering, her hands like ice, and Will was stiff-backed and tense—but there had been no word of apology. They had acted as though there couldn't have been anything to apologize for. They were just warm-hearted regular old grandparents.

When Edna had called the next week and invited them to dinner again, because no one spoke out the truth the first tine, there seemed no reason to say no the second time, and, strangely and easily, they had fallen into this pattern of coming to Sunday dinner. Martha began to accept it as part of her life. A sense of continuity grew out of the visits—taking the baby to her grandparents, being served an elaborate dinner, watching television. She and Will found themselves going without discussing it.

So here they were, with Ed Sullivan bowing out for the last commercial.

Her father-in-law went forward and switched off the set. "So, Will?" he said. "What did you think of the Giants winning?"

Reluctantly, Will put down the papers and showed his face. "I don't care one way or another," he said.

"So what have you been doing on your days off? Taking the baby to the zoo?"

"She's too young."

"So what do you do?"

"We mostly stay home."

"Will's building a record cabinet," Martha volunteered, which was strange, since she usually let the old man founder till he realized that conversation was impossible.

"Is that so? Is that so?" he said. "Tell me about it, Will."

"Nothing to tell. I'm just building it."

"Oh, Harry," Martha said. "Will needs a large screwdriver. You wouldn't happen to have one, would you?"

"Sure, sure I do," Harry said, delighted to be of some use. "I'll find it for you right now. Why didn't you ask sooner? I could have driven over with it." He got up and went into the kitchen.

"It's not important," Will called after him. "I can get one at Woolworth's."

"Not at all, not at all," Harry answered, rattling things in a cabinet. "I know it's here somewhere," he said, his voice muffled.

Will picked up the papers again. It was very quiet without the television. The sound of the running shower could be heard above the thump of Harry's pulling everything out of the kitchen drawers. The baby sat on the rug, rolling an apple against one chubby thigh and back against the other. Martha went over to her husband on the couch and said, "Let him find the screwdriver. Borrow it from him. Thank him, for heaven's sake, Will. Let him do something for us."

Will looked up at her, and then moved forward and rubbed his head in a kind of anguish against her stomach. "Oh Martha," he whispered. "I'm sorry for all this mess."

She felt him lean back quickly at a sound from the bathroom, and to hide her own confusion she began to diaper the baby, holding the pins in her mouth and keeping her head bent.

By the time the bathroom door opened and her mother-in-law came out, her wet hair slicked against her skull, Martha was sitting on the floor, holding the baby against her chest like a shield. Her mother-in-law, with her makeup washed off, and wearing only a robe without her many supporting garments, looked loose and old, worn and tired. "I think we'll have to go soon," Martha said. "It's way past the baby's bedtime. She's going to get cranky any minute."

"Oh, don't go yet," Edna said. "I'll make some coffee. Stay a while."

"Haven't we made enough of a mess for you for one evening?" Martha said with a laugh, indicating the apples on the floor, the crumbs from the baby's zwieback, the chocolatey fingerprints on the yellow plastic elephant that Edna kept in a drawer, to be pulled out when the baby arrived.

"So what?" Edna said. "So what if there's a mess? We're alone all week. That's what we live for." As if she had said more than she meant to, she quickly stooped and ruffled the baby's silky hair with her hand. The baby turned toward her and smiled, without prejudice. Martha saw her mother-in-law move as though to lift the baby, but instead change her direction and awkwardly pick a piece of dirt from the rug.

It occurred to Martha quite suddenly that neither Edna nor Harry ever lifted the baby without first turning to her for permission. In fact, even when they wanted something of Will they asked her first. They would say, "Do you think Will would like more coffee?" or, "Apple pie or apricot pie for Will?" as though they were afraid to act without her consent or approval, and also as if Will's preference for the kind of pie he liked when he was a boy had been automatically voided by his marriage.

"We'd love to stay a little longer, Edna, but really we've got to get home. Will has to get up early, and the baby will be all off schedule if we don't get her in bed soon."

Edna stepped back, nodding her head obediently, and did not plead further.

Clearly now, Martha understood that she was the one in power; the authority for decisions was hers now. They were old and at her mercy. She had their son, she had their grand-child, and she had the power of depriving them of one or both. "Come on, Will," she said. "Let's get all the stuff together and go."

Will, behind his barricade, did not move.

"You think it was easy being his mother?" Edna said, and Martha, oddly moved by this confession, hurried to gather up the baby's toys and clothes and bottles.

In the kitchen she found her father-in-law, sitting on the floor, surrounded by the contents of five cabinets. "I know it's here," he said, "but I can't find it. Maybe I'll look in the car. Maybe it's there." He stepped out of his circle of cans and pots, and went out the door.

When Martha came back into the living room, Will was standing; he had his jacket on. He lifted the baby up toward her, and Martha, taking and balancing the small weight on her hip, wrapped her in her blanket. Edna came toward them and tucked the ends of the blanket more tightly behind the baby, making her snug in the pink envelope. "You made a delicious dinner," Martha said. "You go to so much trouble—we never feast like that at home."

"It's nothing, I enjoy it," Edna said. "Please come soon. During the week if you want to. No need to wait for the weekend."

Will brushed in front of his mother and stood halfway out the door, his hand touching the small of Martha's back to hurry her.

"Why, maybe we will," Martha said. "That might be nice— to come during the week."

Without a word of farewell, Will began to walk toward the car, and Martha, reddening, took the baby's arm out of the blanket and waved it. "Say bye-bye to Grandma."

"Bye-bye, sweet darling," her mother-in-law said to the baby, and then suddenly she said, "Someday my son will kiss me goodbye."

Instinctively, Martha held out the baby to her mother-in-law, and when the old woman's arms folded around her, Martha said, "Can you kiss Grandma goodbye? Can you give a kiss?" She leaned in front of the baby and put her lips against her mother-in-law's cheek. "Like this," she said to the baby. "Can you do it?"

Edna drew Martha against her, and for an instant the two women hugged, the baby between them.

Martha, moving now to follow her husband, looked back at her mother-in-law, and, taking courage from the latitude she had discovered in her soul, she was able to say without strain, "Tell Dad goodbye for us, and if he finds the screwdriver, we'll come and pick it up tomorrow."

# Approval

AFTER DINNER, one by one, Martha's family pushed back their chairs and wandered singly onto the front porch, where the end of the day was just beginning. She heard Will say to her parents something about the rain bringing out the mosquitoes, and then saw him come back into the house and sit down at his desk in the living room.

Tonight had been one of the less fortunate family dinners—Will had been preoccupied with a lecture he was writing, and her father had wanted to discuss an idea he had for a world peace plan: a monumental chain letter, to be sent to every human being in the world, reminding them of the benefits of a peaceful universe. The conversational exchange had been very bare, and Martha's father had finally taken to rolling up bits of bread into little balls and pressing them onto the tablecloth.

She wiped the tomato seeds off the baby's face, and cleaned the highchair, all the while aware of the sounds from the porch—nothing but the squeak squeak of the rusty glider springs. Finally she called, "I'll be out in ten minutes, as soon as I get this little cupcake to bed."

"Take your time," her mother answered. "We're very comfortable."

Martha took the leftover corned beef from the pot and set it on a plate to cool. Then she hoisted the baby on her hip and carried her to the living-room door.

"Say nighty-night to Daddy," she commanded.

"Cookie," the child said obligingly; and before Will, who had turned around in his chair, could bid the baby goodnight, Martha's father called in from the porch, "Sweet dreams, little princess," and then said quite loudly, to his wife, "Babies thrive on affection. Kiss them and feed them—those are the only important things. Young people don't give their youngsters enough affection these days. They don't think it's important."

Martha carried the baby off, unkissed by anyone, to bed, and came back out onto the porch to try to salvage some of the evening. She sat down on the swing between her parents, and, with an exaggerated sigh, pulled her hair away from her neck. It was quite dark, but still very hot.

"We were just talking about that boy your cousin Elizabeth married," her father said. "He was such a warm, good-natured fellow."

"I never met him," Martha said.

"Why doesn't Will come out here where it's cooler?"

"He's preparing a lecture he has to give tomorrow," she said. "They give him a lot of work to do."

In her father's eyes she knew it was a poor excuse, but why should he demand any of her at all? She did not know exactly what he wanted of her. It was clear he did not see just why she had married this boy; but it was also clear that she was already married to him. Evidence enough was the little-princess grand-baby her father loved so dearly—who alone should have mitigated his disapproval to some degree.

Her father was a man who had a philosophy to justify every action. During her teen years, he had stressed again and again,

"What you have to look for in a husband, sweetheart, is a sense of humor, a love of fellow humans, a trust in mankind, and a warm heart. A man without a warm heart is worse than no man at all."

Her mother was less demanding; perhaps she would have appreciated a son-in-law who wired flowers on Mother's Day and greeted her with affectionate kisses, but in the absence of such, she was fairly satisfied with a steady man whom her daughter (for reasons somewhat occult to her, no doubt) seemed happy with.

"They said yesterday was the hottest in four years," Martha said. "I believe it."

"You just live in a hot *section*," her father said. "Here the sun bakes down all day, no buildings, no shade. If you lived more in the city you wouldn't have all these mosquitoes and spiders. I still don't know why you picked this forsaken place out in the sticks. All these insects aren't good for the baby."

"It's pleasant out here," Martha said. "You're not right on top of everybody. You don't have to listen to TV when your neighbor watches the Late Show. You don't have to hear anybody's arguments but your own."

"I don't know how much you and Will argue," her father said, "but I'd rather hear a television than have these trains going by every five minutes, day and night."

As if to corroborate her father's pronouncement, the blasting whistle of the freight train shocked their ears, and they were all quiet while the train crashed and rumbled past the crossing half a block from their door.

"A noise like that could give the baby nightmares," her father said finally when the last sounds of the train had disappeared. "The city is safer, more sensible."

No one was aware of the man until he spoke in the doorway. It gave them all a bad start, Martha especially, because she had just leaned back and closed her eyes.

"I wonder," he said, and he stopped speaking. He was so close to the screen door that Martha heard the hairs of his beard scrape on the wire. Beside her, her father instinctively reached for his back pocket and patted his wallet, a gesture he made twenty times a day.

In the wan light coming from the living room, Martha could see that the man's pants were too long by four inches, and he carried over his arm a torn khaki coat, his only luggage. He was old. His hair, had it been clean, would probably have been white.

No one had moved, and Martha's mother said from her corner, curtly, "What can we do for you?"

The man seemed unable to speak in answer to such a tone of voice. After a moment he said, "Excuse me," and moved his hand toward his hair, in the gesture of one tipping his hat.

"See if the baby's all right," Martha's father said into her ear. "Go on." Martha understood he was suggesting a plot: this man was a decoy. While he fumbled and mumbled here his partner was at the back of the house removing the bedroom screen and kidnapping the baby from her crib.

"She's all right, Dad," she said. "Don't worry." Where all her father's suspicions and fears came from she could not imagine.

The man was beginning to step back from the door. He seemed to be fading out, as though he were being broadcast on a weak signal.

Martha felt a vibration under the porch floor, and first felt, then saw, Will step out onto the porch, his white shirt moving like a beacon in the dark.

"Hello," he said, calling the man back. "Can I *help* you?"

The man came forward again and pressed his hands against the screen, the way a child at a window will do, and he said, "Could I do some work for you? I wonder if you have something for me to do. I can do anything."

Will said, "Let me think a minute." Martha's parents were looking down at their laps She felt their tenseness on either side of her. She heard Will say finally, "I'm very sorry, but I can't think of a single thing you could do right now. I'm going to put up a fence around the house for the baby, but the materials won't be delivered till next week. If you can come by then, I can give you work."

Martha's father leaned toward her and whispered in her ear, "He shouldn't have mentioned the baby! And don't let him encourage him to hang around. He looks like a dangerous character to me. He doesn't want work, he's just looking for a handout."

"Thank you," the old man said to Will. "Thank you, sir. Very much. But I'm afraid I have to move on." He tipped his invisible hat again, and turned around to step down into the darkness. They were all silent as they listened to him walk away over the gravelly front yard and down the road.

Will disappeared into the house without a word, and Martha and her parents sat on the swing, hearing the approach of another train.

"These bums hop freight trains," her father said. "All kinds of characters ride these trains. There's no need for Will to be so polite, with you alone here with the baby most of the time. You ought to get a watchdog."

"Oh Dad!" Martha cried, unable to stop herself. "He was just a harmless old man. Think of what his life must be like."

"Never mind. I *know* what his life must be like. You underestimate your father, you haven't lived as long as me. You just don't encourage individuals who act like that."

"Who act like *what*?" Martha asked in exasperation. "How does he act that's so terrible?"

"Listen to me a minute, Martha. Take my word for it, a man like that is an immoral human being. Do you know who most of these transients are? They're men like me, men with wives and children, who once had a job they went to every day like I do. But they get beaten down, soon they have nothing but pressures—money and insurance and doctors and wives who scream at them all the time. So one day they stop and think. They hate their wives, they hate their jobs, they hate their lives. Their existence is excruciating. They say to themselves, 'What is this life I'm living like a dead one?'—and then they desert. They just walk off, change their names and go on down the road. That harmless old man who just walked off your steps probably left a wife and five children starving somewhere years ago."

"Oh Dad."

"Don't 'oh Dad' me. It's true. Not everyone can stand up to the pressures of modern-day life. Ask your mother."

"There's no sense in talking this way," Martha's mother said. She seemed visibly shaken by what her husband had just said; she seemed to be listening to him on another frequency, as though his message had a separate and private meaning for her.

"Ask your mother," Martha's father insisted. There was a certain desperate hysteria in his voice that Martha at first could not believe was there. What had started this? His eyes were fixed on the black screen in front of him, he seemed to have forgotten entirely about the old man and his lecture concerning safety.

"Ask your mother," he said urgently to the screen. "Ask her what happened to us during the depression when your sister had meningitis and I had to steal apples from produce trucks so we could eat."

"There's no sense in this, Dave," Martha's mother said. "Why turn over old stones to find worms?"

"Because Martha wants to feel sorry for this old tramp. If she needs to feel sorry for someone, maybe she'll feel sorry for me when I tell her I left you and the children and went away, because I gave up, I hated my life."

Martha had known something was coming, but was nonetheless unprepared. She had not known it was this. She had had hints of something dark several times in her childhood, when her mother spoke to her aunts on the phone, or when her parents were having vague, veiled arguments with voices like knife blades—but she had not known it would be this.

Her father's face appeared desperate—she had to touch his arm and say, "Don't worry. It's all right, Dad, you came back."

At her touch, her father seemed to relax—to collapse somehow. "Ah, Martha baby," he said. "Your mother's right. There's no sense. Let's forget about all this talk. Only be careful around here, don't take chances, it's too isolated."

"Yes," her mother said, grateful to be back on a subject she could handle at a safe distance from her own heart, "I didn't realize before how isolated you are out here. I don't think Will considered you when he chose this place."

"Will *always* considers me!" Martha said, and a sudden frightening hopelessness seized her, as it had done at times in her childhood when her parents refused to understand what they could not bear to recognize.

She stood up. "Well, that's that anyway. Our visitor is gone. Why don't we go in and have some coffee? I have to put the meat away, and besides, it's getting too buggy out here for me."

They blinked in the bright kitchen light, and Martha set out some cups while her parents stood around the table.

"Shall I ask Will if he wants some?" her father said.

"Would you please?"

In a moment her father was back, with the report that Will was not in the house. "Does he often just take off like that and leave you alone in the house?"

"Oh, he's probably gone for a walk, Dad. He'll be back in a minute. Here, would you like some angel cake?"

Martha's hand poured a shaky stream of coffee into the white cups. Will had never before left the house without telling her he was going out. Her stomach was beginning to feel hollow and strange—a symptom of fear, and with it came a growing anger at Will, because he had gone out into the dark scary night and frightened her (or had her father frightened her?) and because he was seeming to prove to her father that he *was* inconsiderate. And not only that, but strange, irresponsible, cold-hearted, and unlikeable.

"Maybe Will went out because he wanted to get away for a while. Maybe he feels we come over too often," her father said offhandedly.

"Oh no," Martha said. "He knows it makes me happy to see you. He likes for you to come because he likes me to be happy." It seemed like the wrong thing to say after she had said it, and she felt uncomfortably close to tears.

Unable to hold the full cup in her shaking hand, she excused herself to look in on the baby, and to ascertain that Will was truly not in the house. Then she came back to the kitchen to put away the leftover corned beef. When she discovered it gone—it and the plate—she knew at once why Will had gone out. She shivered a little in relief, and happiness. He was safe. And he was *good*. In a minute they would know how good he was, that she had, after all, married a warm-hearted boy. No monster, her Will—an angel of mercy instead.

And her parents might even have a doubt or two now about the temperatures of their own hearts.

She sat at the table with her parents and sipped her coffee, her ears tuned to the outside of the house. Finally she heard Will's step on the back stairs. In a moment he was standing in the full light of the kitchen, the empty white plate bright in his hand. At the sight of him, Martha flushed with emotion, as though he had said some tender, intimate thing to her, unexpectedly.

Will slid the plate into the sink, and said, to all of them, "It was the best thing I could think of. Maybe he'll find some work tomorrow." He smiled a little shyly, oddly, at them, and then said, "I have to get back to work."

Martha watched his back as he walked toward his desk, the shirt pulled tightly across his shoulders, his arms hanging awkwardly in the certain way they had.

When he was out of hearing, she turned, smiling, to face her parents, and to receive congratulations on her choice of her husband.

"Weren't you planning to have that meat for lunch tomorrow?" her mother asked her, and at first Martha thought she was joking.

"What does Will care *what* Martha was planning," her father said, willing to take off from any point. "What does he care at all? He walks out at night and leaves Martha alone with the baby in the house with all sorts of characters lurking around here, he goes out after a bum to give him meat meant for the baby's lunch, a bum who could have had a gun and killed him and left Martha a widow. What does Will care about anything?"

"The man was *hungry*, Dad."

"Every man is hungry for something," her father said. "All I want is for my daughter to be taken care of. Will has no sense of responsibility. He doesn't even have life insurance to protect you. He could die tomorrow and then what? He has too much sympathy for bums, believe me. He tells them to come back next week. He tells them he has a baby who'll be out loose in the yard, alone, soon. He has too much understanding and sympathy for that way of life. Tell me, Martha, how do you know he won't walk out the door tomorrow and never come back? How do you know he won't get on one of these freight trains? How do you know it isn't too much for him, writing all these lectures, paying for a house, getting the baby ten-dollar shoes every few weeks? How do you know?"

It was so ludicrous, it was so terrible, that Martha could no longer refuse to respond violently; they had forced her into their broiling hot center again—in the same senseless way they had done during her girlhood when she had no resources at all to protect herself against them.

She answered her father through the beginning of tears. "Will isn't going to desert us, Dad, he wants to *keep* us. He *wants* us—he likes to write his lectures and to pay for the baby's shoes because he *wants* us."

She looked up into her father's flushed face, and saw from the expression around his mouth that he was about to begin a new chain of accusations against Will. She did not try to stop the words that rose to her lips: "You deserted us not because your life was so hard, but because you didn't *want* us!"—and then ran weeping to the baby's room where she knelt by the baby's rocking horse, and rested her hot face on the plastic saddle.

It was not fair, it was not *fair* for them to come here and involve her in their failures; it was not fair that she still was expected to take their difficulties as her own. In this house—her house—she ought not to have to be a victim any longer.

The springs on the rocking horse creaked slightly as her weight shifted and the baby sighed, turning in the crib so that her small hand fell out between the bars and hung there in the air.

Martha went toward the crib and moved downward to place her cheek against the baby's warm hand. She and Will loved this baby so much—they were so happy to have her—how could her father not have wanted his children? She had not meant it when she had said to him, "It's all right, you came back"—the shock of his confession was still ringing in her.

She heard a chair scrape on the floor, and then the sound of her father coming down the hall, her mother's footsteps an echo behind him. They came through the doorway cautiously, her mother on tiptoe to see over her father's shoulder, and to keep her heels from tapping on the floor.

In the dim green glow of the night-light they made their way around the baby's toys, and came to stand beside Martha at the crib. They waited there awkwardly, looking at the child...and looking to Martha's eyes very old.

"I've been thinking about what you said, Martha," her father said finally. "Maybe what you said was right. Maybe when I went away I didn't want you and your mother and your sister anymore. Maybe I was thinking only of myself."

Beside him, Martha's mother's head was down, her eyes focused blindly on some point in the crib.

"The world is different now. It's a different place to live in. Your Will is a different man than I am. My mistake is—I'm still afraid of the world the way it was, the way *I* was. My mistake is—I shouldn't try to make everyone see it the way I do." He moved his hands back and forth across the baby's crib railing.

"Your sister wasn't much older than this little one, Martha. We thought she was dying, her temperature was a hundred and five. We had no heat in the house, no food. Your mother was...beside herself."

Martha's mother did not look up. Her father took his hand from the rail and placed it lightly on his wife's back, partly in accusation, partly in protection. "Your mother said that if Joan died it would be my fault. She was nearly wild, sitting up all night with that burning baby, so I made it that much worse. I left in the middle of it all. I just walked out. I don't know why your mother took me back."

A vague memory of that winter rose in Martha's mind like the frost that iced up on the windows in the porch that had been her bedroom. If *her* baby was dying, Will would never leave. No matter what. No matter if they were all naked and starving. But then she would never say to him, "If the baby dies it will be your fault." She looked suddenly at her mother's bowed head and realized that the flaws could not all be assigned to her father. Whatever the condition of that special world, there had just not been enough love, enough approval, in their feelings for one another to tide them over. Martha believed, reaching back from her comfortable life to that bleak stretch of time which had left so great a mark on the world, that any crisis in life could be weathered if two people approved each other's actions through the worst of it. There had to be some trust—and in her parents' home there had been only recriminations, goads, accusations, threats. She remembered...and from her parents' present misery she knew they could not forget either.

Martha touched her father's hand. "Mother took you back because you *came* back, Dad. Don't you see—it's not as bad as you think, because you *did* come back. You decided you *did* want us. Everything is all right now," and as she said it this time, she meant it urgently.

The cloud on her father's face cleared as she spoke. "Of course," he said. "Of *course* I did."

Martha put her arms around him and hugged him, and he squeezed her so hard she gasped, laughing. Her mother came and took her hand and the three of them stood smiling together in their unexpected reunion until the baby refused to ignore further commotion, and protested with a resentful wail.

Martha swung her from the crib and nuzzled her neck. "You know," she said, "Will and I think she looks like you, Dad, especially when she laughs."

"Is that right?" her father said. "Is that right?"

"And she looks like Mother when she's grumpy!"

Satisfied with the smile she elicited from her mother, Martha deposited the baby on her father's shoulder, and went from the room.

She would not trouble them further by instructing them in the reasons she saw for their failures; there was no sense in it, it was perhaps too late. But too late only for them.

She went into the living room where Will sat at his desk in front of the uncurtained window, bathed in a cone of radiance from his reading lamp. In unhindered view of any and all dangerous characters lurking in the tall grasses, Martha surprised him with full and lengthy measure of her approval.

# Honeymoon

O N THEIR WAY OUT of the Bun Boy coffee shop in Baker, Rand gave Cheryl a quarter to buy a Bio-Rhythm fortune card from a vending machine. She stood in the hot desert wind, her skirt lashing about her legs like a whip, strands of hair flying into her mouth, while she laughingly read him the news that the bio-graph rated her low on luck, low on sex, and low on leisure plans, while it rated her high on health, endurance, and driving.

"So can I drive the rest of the way to Vegas now?" she asked. "It's so boring just to look out the window. There's no scenery."

"Get in the car, please," Rand said, his pants legs flapping like banners in a used-car lot, "...and don't put another ding in my door."

"I didn't put the first ding in," she said, getting into his red Corvette. She automatically took a sip of water from the insulated cup hanging in a holder on the dash and made a face. "Yuck—hot."

"You just had a milkshake," Rand said. "Why do you have to drink old water?"

"I don't know," she said shrugging. "I just saw it there. Don't worry about it."

He pulled onto the road, and up ahead of them Cheryl saw white pompoms on a car. "I wish *we* could have a 'Just Married' sign," she said. "Then everyone would look in *our* car when they passed us."

Rand accelerated, and Cheryl peered into the car with the pompoms. The girl, a blonde like her, turned her head the other way when she saw Cheryl staring. The boy, who looked about the age of Rand's son, gave her a zany grin, friendly and lewd at the same time. Cheryl waved, giggling out loud. She turned to Rand, seeing his handsome profile against the twisted Joshua trees in the distance. "How could I be low on sex and leisure plans if this is my honeymoon?" she asked. She reached over and stroked his thigh. "Anyway, I've *never* been low on sex."

"How do you rate on money?" Rand asked.

"They don't have money on the chart," Cheryl said, consulting the card. "But it says that today is a triple-critical day for me."

"Then stay away from the slots."

"Are you kidding? Last time we went to Vegas I got three bars twice!"

"Play blackjack," he said, "the odds are better."

"Sure, the way *you* do it. If I could count cards, I'd walk away with a few thousand dollars every time, too."

"Even without counting," Rand said, "the game gives you better odds than the slots."

"I always do something wrong," she said. "I hit when I should stand, I stand when I should hit...."

"Memorize the chart I gave you. It tells you exactly what to do."

"It's too hard," she said. "I can't memorize the chart. I'd rather play the slots."

"Well—at least stick around for the first hour or two to play for me. They know me in most places, but they don't know you yet."

"Do I have to play even on my honeymoon?"

"Of course," Rand said. "You don't want them to give me trouble, do you?"

They had a system. If Rand placed his chips to the left side of the circle, it meant Cheryl should hit. (Cheryl remembered this by thinking that if she was left back a grade, she was bad and should be hit.) The chips placed to the right meant she should stand and not take any cards. (She remembered this by thinking that when her answer was right, she would stand at the front of the class and everyone would applaud.) If Rand put his elbow on the table she was supposed to double down on her bet. If he reached into his pocket for his handkerchief, it meant she should bet a hundred dollars. If he took out his wallet and looked inside it, she was to bet *five hundred dollars.*

She felt important, having hundred-dollar chips on the table in front of her, and she loved it when he didn't make errors and they won big. Afterward he'd be so energetic and high, swinging her around in their room, making good love instead of letting her do all the work, later taking her to "Spice on Ice," or some other flashy midnight show, both of them all dressed up. She adored the glitter—the massive headdresses, the pastel doves flying across the room, the seminude ice-skating—the glory and pageantry of it all. Rand wasn't interested in the dancers—even with their breasts hanging out of the costumes with cut-out fronts. He said he didn't think women marching around in circles on a stage were erotic. What he liked were the really dirty movies, which turned Cheryl on but made her feel slightly sick. She didn't need sick movies to be turned on, she was only nineteen and her blood pulsed at the slightest invitation, her dreams were lush with limbs and lips and loving whispers. But Rand said the movies were good for him; he needed to get a little charge now and then.

When she'd called home with the news, her mother had been hurt and angry. Cheryl was really surprised because her mother was tough and had always made fun of big affairs with strolling violinists and airplanes that flew by with flashing bulbs that spelled out "Congratulations on your marriage." She'd phoned from outside the Van Nuys courthouse to tell her parents she'd just been married, and her mother had said, "That's nice, I suppose," and then was absolutely silent. Cheryl almost said, "You didn't really want to be there, did you?" but thought better of it. Her mother didn't ask her a single question—like who was there, or what kind of ring he gave her, or which dress did she wear—so Cheryl finally volunteered into the silence that they were going to Las Vegas for their honeymoon.

"A work-play vacation?" her mother said. "How convenient for him."

"Can you put Daddy on?" Cheryl asked, wobbling in the phone booth on four-inch-high black heels. In the courthouse, she had turned her ankle coming up the stairs, wearing those heels. Rand liked her to wear that kind of shoe—he had bought her half a dozen pairs.

"Daddy's busy," her mother had said.

"Well—wish us luck," Cheryl said, wishing she didn't have to beg.

"In Vegas...or for life?" her mother asked.

"Fuck it," Cheryl had answered, hanging up the phone. Maybe she hung up the phone first and then said it, she couldn't remember, with Rand standing there impatiently in his striped suit, his hair—still thick but at least half-gray—riffling in the breeze. She didn't bother to cry. Rand had no patience with her when she acted like a baby.

"Well, that takes care of your folks. They give you a bad time?" he asked, seeing her face.

"That's okay," she said, "it doesn't matter. Don't you want to call your son now?"

"Not really," Rand said.

"Well, he's the one that had a fit that we were living together."

"He'll find out," Rand said. "Let's just forget about them all right now and get this show on the road."

"Look what I got in the rest room of the coffee shop," Cheryl said as they drove along. "Mr. Hiram's Super Funbook with three free meals."

"Just what we need," Rand said. "Sirens in your ears, hookers bumping asses with you, and sexy Chinese girls patting the dollar slots, whispering 'Try this one, it's hot.'"

"At Mr. Hiram's they give you a free color photo," Cheryl said. "On one of our trips I went in there without you, and I got a picture of my face on a fake dollar bill, and a free phone call home."

"I can give you all the change you need," Rand said, "assuming you want to call home again."

"I don't. Believe me, I don't. But maybe it would be nice to get the free picture. Sort of a wedding picture."

"I've had enough of those already," Rand said. "Don't you think three is enough?"

"How about later on, maybe we can ask someone to take just one snapshot of us with my Polaroid?"

"Maybe," Rand said. "We'll see."

Cheryl stared for a while out the window at the spiky yucca plants and the knobby dwarfed trees. "I wonder if we'll have a room with a mirror this time," she said. "I wonder if we'll have fun."

"Don't we always?" Rand said.

Her best girlfriend had a job now doing word processing for ten dollars an hour. In high school they had talked about going on to junior college and studying computers, but in the end her friend got on-the-job training on a Wang and now worked in downtown LA for an engineering company.

Cheryl had taken a summer job at Saks, gift wrapping, and in the fall decided to stay with it a while until she had a clearer idea of what she wanted to do. Her mother and father seemed relieved that they weren't going to have to fork over five thousand a year to send her to some fancy college, and as long as she was paying her own gas and insurance on the '71 Ford they let her use, they didn't bother her. That is, until she met Rand—he was having a birthday present gift-wrapped for his third wife—and started seeing him every night. Then her parents started babbling all the usual stuff: "more than twice your age, after you because you're a gorgeous young girl, you ought to be dating his sons!"

What did they know? The guys her own age were nothing, invisible, scarecrows on hangers. They glugged beer and walked to some drumbeat in their heads; she was sick of faded jeans and running shoes and guys who couldn't wait to turn you on with grass or with their own throbbing bodies. They had no money, and never would. Times were getting so crazy that they all had to live with their parents, no one could afford the rent on an apartment, even sharing with two or three guys. Half of the guys she knew thought they would be famous rock stars; they couldn't even carry a tune.

Rand was a real person. He had a science degree, he had been an engineer or something for many years till he got sick of it. His kids, from his different wives, were all grown up, and he was sending his youngest son through college now. He really knew where it was at. He never told dumb jokes. He didn't play games. He said what he wanted and she liked that. Do this, do that—and she did it, because usually it was a better idea than anything she could think of herself.

Now with their luggage carried in, he tipped the bellboy and locked the door of their room.

"Call room service and order us each a big shrimp cocktail," Rand said, his body reflected a dozen times in the mirrored room as he hung up his clothes in the alcove.

"I don't know if I want that," Cheryl said. "Maybe I want a hamburger."

"Call! Call!" he said. "Hurry up. When I get out of the shower I want it to be here."

And when it came, big white shrimp with pink tails and pink veins arched in a goblet over a snowball of ice, heads swimming in luscious red cocktail sauce, she knew he was right. It was exactly what she wanted. She chewed in a luxury of wanting the shrimp, grateful to him. When he came out of the shower she had eaten half of his shrimp, too—and he looked at the bloody plate and laughed, and peeled off his damp towel and swatted her. "That's what I love about you," he said. "Your healthy appetites. All of them."

By the time they got to the casino, she was quite satisfied, and chewed her lip comfortably while she adored him. She sat two stools down from him at the blackjack table, and felt his concentration burning toward her, his eyes counting the cards, figuring out when a ten-card would come up, knowing how many aces were left to fall at his—or the dealer's—place. The dealer was "Nancy from Indiana"—a sweet-faced, red-headed girl with heavy black eye makeup. He was joking with her, and tilting his toes, and counting cards at the same time. He was really brilliant. He won three forty-dollar bets in a row and bantered with the dealer: "It's not how you play the game, but whether you win or lose." The girl didn't get it. Cheryl hadn't gotten it the first time he'd said it either, but later he explained it to her and now she thought it was a funny joke. He took his handkerchief out of his pocket now, and Cheryl bet one hundred dollars on the next hand. It came up a ten and a jack, and she didn't even watch for his signal as he slid his chips to the right; she was catching on, she knew she had to stand with a twenty, it didn't matter what the dealer had.

Bad luck! The dealer had blackjack. Nancy-from-Indiana swept the chips away, click, click, click, just like that, not caring for the narrowness of his eyes, the ugly clenching of his jaw muscles. This was what Cheryl hated, when it didn't go his way and his temper got foul.

She played the next three hands at his instruction, and twice he was wrong again. He had lost his concentration. He scooped up his remaining chips, raised an eyebrow at her, and walked to the keno lounge. After playing two token hands to establish that she was separate from him, in case the pit boss was watching, Cheryl met him there. He was adding some figures on a keno sheet, writing with thick black crayon.

"Why don't you ever play bingo with me?" she said. "I think that would be fun." The kind of look he gave her made her want to race away, to run all the way back to LA, to see her mother, even to go to junior college. She abruptly left him, saying she was going to the rest room.

A black woman in a uniform was mopping up leaks from the faucets with hotel towels. "You know how the engineers make these hotels," she said to Cheryl. "Every minute this place don't go up in flames, I thank God."

But the mirrors were perfect. They had the right kind of pink light coming down that always made her skin look especially creamy and smooth. She smiled at herself, a flash of a smile that was brilliant. Sometimes she really *was* gorgeous and she felt proud. When she stood at bus stops, her thick blonde hair blowing around her face, she impressed the traffic, she knew that.

"You winning, honey?" the black lady asked. Cheryl saw her white plate waiting, empty of tips.

"Yeah, I'm really lucky tonight," she said, digging in her big red nylon purse and putting a twenty-five-dollar chip on the plate. "This is my honeymoon."

"No kidding," the lady said. "How about that?"

Cheryl went out into the casino again, into the smoke and the clatter of silver dollars and the raucous shouts coming from the craps table. She saw Rand's rounded back hunched at another table; he was playing again. She wandered around to the slot carousel, got twenty silver dollars, and idly put them in a machine, three at a time, to buy all three payoff lines. The last pull she only had two to put in, and son of a gun, the three bars showed up on the bottom line and she hadn't paid for them. Shit, she hated that. It happened once before and she didn't get three hundred quarters. Things like that could make her cry. She couldn't believe she would cry over something like that. Yet she was filling up, her nose and eyes, and she wanted to say to God, How come not me? How come everyone else is so lucky, only not me? Right next to her a young couple, maybe twenty-two or twenty-three, had two ice buckets filled with silver dollars. As she watched they hit another jackpot and the girl yelled, "O-*kay*!" and the guy gave her a big hug. Cheryl checked to see if the girl had a wedding ring. She did, and an engagement ring, too. Cheryl looked at her own wedding band. Already she didn't like it; she had picked the wrong one this morning. They had been in too much of a hurry, trying to squeeze in a wedding and a trip to Vegas in the same day. Rand had said he would buy her a diamond if they had a big hit this weekend. The high rollers all bought their women jewelry. Sometimes the wives took half the winnings right off the table, cashed in the chips, and went straight to the jewelry store to buy gold bracelets. Cheryl would never have the nerve to scoop up half of Rand's winnings. Maybe she just hadn't been married long enough.

Now an old man on her other side hit three oranges and stood back, chewing on a cigar, while thirty coins clanged down into the tin bowl. he put three more dollars in the slot, and three bars turned up, giving him a hundred more. He looked around for something to do while the bells rang and the money arrived, and said to Cheryl, "You using this machine?"

"No, you can have it," she said, stepping back, and she felt a few tears wash over the edge of her eye.

"Hey, hey," the old man said. "You lose everything?"

She nodded.

"Then take a handful of mine. Go ahead, I won't feel it. I have oil wells."

"I don't think so," Cheryl said. "I have to quit now."

"Here," he insisted. "Just fill up a bucket."

"It doesn't work that way," Cheryl said. "I don't think you can use someone else's luck." She went out to the lobby to look at the waterfall. A new bride was standing there, a young Mexican girl with flowers on her wrist. Her husband, a handsome Latino with a pencil mustache, wearing a white jacket, came over to Cheryl and said, "Could you take a picture of us, please?" He handed her his camera. "Just push here."

They were both children, Cheryl thought. Men her own age were really children, weren't they? She took a picture they would keep forever, but they would never remember her standing there, taking it. She knew she would always remember them.

"We appreciate it," the girl said, the water crashing down behind her, sending up a rainbow spray of dots against the rocks. To their retreating backs Cheryl said, "I wish I had a wedding picture. I just got married, too."

Deciding to go back to the hotel room, she crossed the pool area and saw a Hawaiian luau in progress. Four black-haired girls in flowered red dresses were dancing a hula on a wooden platform. The music was very serene and dreamy; the girls' hands were as delicate as birds. Their hips slid slowly back and forth under their long dresses as if they were under water. Cheryl knew she would never be that peaceful. She stood on the damp grass and watched, feeling the tears come again. Then she took the elevator up to their room and fell asleep.

"Butterflies, Love-Lites, roses, cigars...." The cigar girl passed their table in the coffee shop and Cheryl tapped her on the back. The girl swung around, her long stockinged legs seeming to take up most of her body.

"Are those Love-Lites you're wearing?" Cheryl asked. "How do they work?" The girl wore flashing red lantern earrings, a blinking red pendant, and a blinking butterfly pin.

"Little hearing-aid batteries," the girl said. "They last forever."

"Could you get me one, Rand?" Cheryl asked, smiling at him.

"Sure," he said. He was composed again, shaved and smelling of Brut. "If you like…." He took out his wallet. "How much?"

"Twenty-five," the girl said, "if you want the Love-Lite earrings."

Cheryl imagined that if she were ever in a dark tunnel, the Love-Lites would light her way to safety. She took off her little ivory elephant earrings and attached the new ones to her ears.

They finished eating their breakfast. She and Rand were in the hotel with a huge gold-colored pot outside—about fifty feet high with a fake ugly rainbow coming up to it.

"Cheap," Cheryl had remarked as they turned into the parking lot. "It makes the whole idea cheap. Now whenever I see a rainbow I'll be reminded of this brassy pot and this ugly rainbow. And when I hear 'Over the Rainbow' I'll think of smoky rooms and bad bets."

"Maybe you'll think of mirrored rooms and piles of money."

"Same thing," Cheryl said.

"Well, let's get going. I could use you to play for me this morning."

"I don't really want to," she said. "I want to do something else. You're safe. They don't know you here, do they? It's a new hotel."

"I suppose I could get along without you for a while. But not tonight."

"I'll play for you tonight, then."

"And do what all day?"

"Who knows?" she said. "Go to Hoover Dam maybe."

As soon as she got on the tour bus she felt a little better. The casinos always seemed like churches to her, with people praying for grace all over the place. You could feel it when you passed a bingo room, the hush, the living prayer, as they all waited to be chosen. In Vegas, to pray and to play was the same thing: you could get saved, you could get lucky. Only the difference was, if God gave you grace, no one lost. In Vegas, if you won, you were just ruining the next guy.

Cheryl leaned her face into the air-conditioning slit under the window. The bus was filling up with lots of elderly ladies. She never wanted to be one of them, with their bluish hair and their pointy eyeglasses. They looked like old birds, all the same. How did they ever have any fun? Sometimes Rand looked like an old bird with his skinny shins, the way the skin on his legs seemed scaly. She was glad he was cooped up in some casino, in the dark daytime inside of those places. She was going out into the sun…where she could thaw out.

She was definitely feeling better. She looked out the window as the bus crossed the desert and she decided there *was* scenery out there. She saw pinkish clay rock formations, and long sandy stretches of browns and beiges and pinks. It looked like a painting. Some clouds were lining up overhead, so it didn't seem quite as hot or bright. Sometimes she thought she had seen everything, thought everything she was ever going to see or think, and the next eighty years of her life were going to be exactly the same as the first twenty. But once in a while she saw something new and got a different feeling, and when that happened, it gave her hope again. At first, being with Rand had given her a thousand new thoughts and feelings, but now she was having no new ones. Like everything else, it had gotten old—and she had only married him yesterday. If, as her mother said, the marriage—considering his record—was sure to be a short-term thing, then *that* was rotten. And if it was to be forever, till death did they part, that seemed rotten, too.

When she first started living with Rand, her mother had said, "Just don't come back home to us with a baby for me to take care of for you." It never occurred to her that she might have a baby with Rand. One of his sons' wives was pregnant. He didn't seem like the type of husband you'd want to have a baby with, a man who already was going to be a grandfather.

"Hoover Dam up ahead," the bus driver announced. "When we park, please line up at the second tower on the Nevada side."

As soon as she got out of the bus, Cheryl found herself behind a young couple in black motorcycle jackets. They each had one hand stuck in the butt pocket of the other's jeans. The girl, curvy and very cute, had long fuzzy black hair, while the guy was tall and good-looking, and wore pointy lizard-skin boots. Cheryl admired his dark wavy hair. When he turned to look down at the river, Cheryl saw a toothpick in his mouth. He made her heart leap, giving out that kind of raw sexiness that did something to her. She wished she were his girl. For a minute, she would have given anything to be that girl.

Blocks of tourists, maybe twenty at a time, were allowed to board the elevator. For five minutes at a time the line came to a stop. Every time it stopped, the guy took the toothpick out of his mouth and kissed his girl, bending her backward passionately. Once the girl looked behind her, embarrassed, and smiled apologetically at Cheryl.

"That's okay," Cheryl said, "I don't mind. I think love is great." She walked behind them as they inched toward the elevator, and looked down the vast sloping side of the dam, which curved downward to the Colorado River, a greenish strip far below them. Tiny dots—birds—flew and lifted against the concrete curve. Cheryl realized that a person could easily kill himself by jumping off here. She had also noticed that it would be easy from the parking garage of The Mint, seventh level, and filed away the information in her head. Most public places tried to keep you from killing yourself, putting up high fences or barbed wire, but then there were other places that didn't seem to worry about the possibility. Right here, at Hoover Dam, you could just get up on the waist-high railing and jump down into the curving concrete side of the dam. If she ever really needed to do it, it would be a long ride from LA.

The motorcycle couple moved along with the line. Now the guy, wearing a black T-shirt under his leather jacket with the words "Harley Davidson, Denver, Colo, USA" on it, had his hand under his girl's belt line and was pressing down to bare skin, as far as he could get under the tight jeans.

"Hey," the girl whispered to him, peeking over her shoulder at Cheryl, "don't do that." The guy turned around and winked at Cheryl. "Hey, you come here too, sweetheart. I have two hands; I can do you both at once." Cheryl laughed and took a step forward, and then the guy had his arm around her, too. The girl laughed and he laughed and the line began to move forward quickly, so she crowded into the elevator with them, and the three of them descended into the mountain, 528 feet down, clinging together.

They walked through a long tiled tunnel behind their guide, a short man with a booming voice who assured them the tunnel did not leak. It was cold in the tunnel and the lights above them were very dim. Now and then the bulbs would black out for a few seconds. Cheryl could feel the thrumming vibration of machinery all around her. "The walls of the dam are 107 feet thick," the guide said. "It is 726 feet high." She was still wrapped in the arm of the guy in the motorcycle jacket. "If you've heard rumors that men were trapped in the concrete, put your minds at ease. The cement here was poured eighteen inches at a time, so it could cure, and you can't lose a man in eighteen inches of concrete. *However*, it *is* true that ninety-six workers were killed between 1931 and 1937: twenty-four fell to their deaths, three drowned, ten were killed by explosions, five were electrocuted, twenty-six were struck by falling debris, twenty-six were struck by machinery, one died in the elevator, and one in a cableway accident."

The girl who was sharing her guy with Cheryl shivered. "How creepy," she said. "What if we get stuck down here?"

"Don't worry," Cheryl offered. "I have my Love-Lites." She held back her hair and showed the girl the glowing lanterns swinging from her ears. "If anything goes wrong, they'll light our way out of here." The girl reached over and took her hand tightly. "How neat," she said. "We're so lucky to have you. This place spooks me."

Cheryl changed places with the guy so that she was between him and the girl; she held hands with both of them going down the long tunnel. In the powerhouse they saw the row of immense electric generators that took the river water and turned it into electricity. The guide gave them a thousand figures, and while he told them how many acres the lake covered, how many kilowatts the power plant produced, Cheryl noticed some little metal machines that resembled robots, funny round tubs with bleeping antennae. She pointed them out to the girl, who squeezed her hand tighter and giggled. "This is so much fun," she said. "I'm so glad we found you."

"Want me to take a picture of you two with my Polaroid?" Cheryl asked, hunting in her nylon bag for her camera. They were being led now through a diversion tunnel, a long dark passage made of volcanic rock ten to fifteen million years old, through which water had run while the dam was being built. The three of them let the tour group pass by them, and then stood alone in the black tunnel. The rocky sides dripped moisture from condensation, and as in a subway train, the lights flickered and went out. From far down the passageway they could hear the gasps and delighted fright of the tourists, and the guide's reassuring voice. Cheryl stood secure in the pinkish glow of her Love-Lites, her new friends gathered close to her. She arranged them against the jagged wall and let her flash explode.

"Want us to take a picture of you?" the girl asked.

"That would be real nice," Cheryl said. "This is sort of a special occasion for me—I've been wishing someone would take a picture of me all day."

"Couldn't you ask anyone?" the girl said.

"Not really," Cheryl said. "I'm out here by myself." Just as she tore the finished picture from the camera and handed it over to them, the lights flashed on, illuminating the three of them in a ring of whiteness. "Look," she said to the guy, "I even got your boots in the picture."

He laughed. "I guess you know what counts," he said. "Here, let me take you now." He posed her against the rock, and she tossed her hair back to let her lanterns shine out. While they were waiting for the print, her friends told Cheryl that they were staying in a camper parked at some strip hotel, and were heading for Zion in the morning.

"Say," the guy said, "if you're traveling alone, maybe you'd like to come along with us for a while." He put his hand on his girl's shoulder and said, "How's that for an idea?"

The girl looked at him. "Well, I guess we could squeeze her in."

"Sure," he said, "the more the merrier."

Cheryl, her back against the rough wall, felt as if the gates of the dam had just been opened, and she was being swept out to sea on the emerald waters.

"Will you do it?" he asked. The girl had taken out an Afro comb and was picking at her fuzzy curls, standing a little away from them.

"Yeah...sure. I will! It sounds great."

"Where are you staying?" he asked. "We'll have to come by and get your luggage."

But just then there was a last warning call for the elevator going up, and because she couldn't run fast on her high heels, they got way ahead of her making a dash down the tunnel. Dancing with impatience, Cheryl had to wait for the second trip up. When she got to the surface they were gone. She walked frantically from the tower on the Nevada side to the tower on the Arizona side, and searched for them in the crowd near the statues of the Winged Figures of the Republic at the entrance to the dam. She heard a faint buzz reverberating off the canyon walls, and in the distance saw the little ant of their motorcycle climbing the hairpin road toward the desert.

Finally she joined the crowd of old ladies going back to the tour bus, and when she found a seat she settled down to study her wedding picture. It was just her luck, she thought, that even the Love-Lites didn't shine out in it. They hung there, like charred corks, from her ears.

# See Bonnie & Clyde Death Car

A T MIDNIGHT, when the temperature in the Sahara Tower registers 102 degrees, two ducks make a landing on the Astroturf around the pool and slip silently into the water. The moon, lying on the pool's surface like a tiny frozen marble, remains undisturbed.

Lynn, who is reclining on a white plastic lounge chair, finds all of this astonishing: the searing heat at midnight, the magical appearance of the ducks (where did they come from? why don't they react to the powerful chlorine fumes rising from the water?), the immutability of the moon's image, her lack of hunger. Do the laws of physics and biology not apply in Las Vegas?

Phil has been at the same blackjack table from the moment they stumbled into the casino from the oven of the parking lot at four P.M.; neither of them has eaten anything since they shared a container of blueberry yogurt after noon, just beyond Barstow, while traveling at seventy-five miles an hour past deformed Joshua trees and empty lake beds. When the plastic spoon broke, Lynn had scooped the purple cream into Phil's mouth with her finger.

She had been to Las Vegas once, five years before, with another man, and had vowed never to come again because it seemed to her the place to end things. At least she had come to the end of her money then, and to the end of her friendship with the man.

Now she is here by default; Phil's suitcase had been packed for another kind of trip, to visit his father in San Francisco, where three days before he had been paralyzed by a stroke. Lynn had desperately not wanted to go with Phil, to attend at yet another hospital bedside. For the last month—till the funeral last Wednesday—she had spent nearly every evening beside the bed of a friend dying of AIDS, a man who had worked at her newspaper and with whom she often had lunch. Since then (she knew it wasn't rational) her fear of illness had assumed phobic proportions. Just when she most needed a rest from facing the void, Phil wanted her along. "I want you with me through thick and thin," he said. "In sickness and health," he added. The words seemed significant to her, so, hopefully, she packed her suitcase. Except that just as they were walking out the door there was a phone call from Phil's mother. They each picked up an extension.

"Don't come now, wait until Dad is stabilized, the doctor thinks a week or so later would be better. We'll know more then, anyway."

When Phil put down the phone, his face was soft and miserable. "God—I'm all packed. What am I supposed to do *now*?" He was holding his car keys in his hand.

"We could always just go on vacation for the weekend," she said. "As long as we get back in time for work on Monday."

He stared at her peculiarly; his expression was unreadable and her heart skipped a beat.

"Phil, listen—that's only a joke, a joke," she apologized.

"No," he said. "You're right. Why not? Why don't we go to Vegas?"

"Why not, I suppose," she said. She sank down into the bean-bag chair she'd claimed on her last trip to see her parents. The beads slid suddenly under her like quicksand. How fast life's direction could change. "Do you think we can get a hotel room?"

A roulette wheel was bolted to the reception desk at the Sahara. The clerk told Lynn to give it a spin to see if she could win a free or half-price room.

"Oh, too bad. Give it another whirl and see if you can do better," the woman urged after Lynn's spin had landed the pointer on the regular room rate. But even with a second chance Lynn got only $2.50 off.

Phil was looking with longing toward the noisy, red-lit casino, leaning his arms on the reception desk. The angle at which his head was reflected in the mirrored wall showed her how thin his hair was getting, how his sideburns (he still wore them) were of slightly different lengths. Well, why did she persist in noting these things? She knew his flaws, his habits, his limits; they were certainly not new to her. She wanted to marry this man; she would rush with him across the street to the Chapel of Happy Memories right now if she could get him to agree. Did it ever occur to him how she cared for him? To the point of requesting a hotel room no higher than the third or fourth floor? Further than that (she had read) the ladders of firemen did not reach.

She saw herself in the mirror—not a glamorous woman, no longer so young. Phil was an unambitious man; worried, nervous, steady, old beyond his years. But she wanted him. It was this knowledge which shaped her mind these days.

After spending hours in the casino, she has come out here to the pool to find quiet. The pair of ducks glide in parallel lines for short distances, then turn and return to where they started from. One of them lets a pellet drop from his body; it snakes through the green water, falling slowly. The two birds glide and turn, glide and turn. They could be swans, they are so graceful. Lynn thinks ahead to mid-morning tomorrow, when the heat will distort the air and the Sahara Tower will show a temperature of 110; who will ever guess that wild creatures swam here last night?

Lynn and a woman have a tug-of-war over a stool between two rows of slot machines, but she relents and lets her have it because she's older than Lynn and looks poor. However, the woman is playing a twenty-five-cent slot while Lynn is taking her chances with only nickels. She definitely is afraid to play quarters; she's already bought one roll of quarters, ten dollars for forty—and, at five coins a pull (she believes in playing for the highest wins as long as she's playing), she gets only eight pulls and the money's gone. No, she can't throw away ten dollars that fast. Silver dollars would be worse. They'd shoot away and turn to quicksilver in the molten heat of the machines.

For a while she stands at Phil's shoulder as he makes bets with two five-dollar chips at a time, sometimes four, but that's his privilege; he's in another sphere, his father is newly para-lyzed. He's entitled to play for high stakes. When he loses two hands in a row, she fears she's changing his luck and wanders away, up and down the aisles of lit and beckoning machines.

She tries a video slot: "I'm loose as a goose," the screen tells her as she puts three nickels in and pulls the arm. Nothing lines up. The machine announces, in red letters, "Game's over. But you look like a winner. Columbus took a chance. Try again." This time three bells show up on the center line and, for a moment, the bells turn into the smiling mustachioed faces of little men—then ten nickels come tumbling down into the tin bowl. Lynn is pleased even though by now a muscle in her right shoulder is burning and her fingers are black from handling the coins. She's getting good at breaking open packets of nickels; expertly she knocks the roll on the lip of the bowl. When it splits, she pushes out the coins from either end with her two index fingers. She's fast. She can put five nickels into a machine without missing a beat; she can put them in *two* machines and pull the handles at once, doubling her chances at the big hit. She enjoys certain diversions she practices (she thinks they are her own invention). For instance, if she drops a coin on the floor, she will wait till the reels are spinning and then kneel to retrieve it. It's her hope that she'll hit a jackpot (without even watching for one) and the machine will spit out a stream of money; she wants to be down there, on her knees, to see her fortune come out of the spout. She wants to be eye-to-eye with her luck as it pours out at her like a silver waterfall.

It's so late that she's lightheaded, feeling weird. There are no clocks in the casino. In the cocktail lounge a Madonna look-alike stands in front of an electronic keyboard singing, "I'm going to keep my baby." Her cleavage shimmers, but it looks innocent on her thin body. The floor vibrates from deep inside. Despite the music, the shouts from the craps tables, the clack of the wheel-of-fortune, the shrieks of the jackpot winners, Lynn feels as she once did at a church service, when a Bach organ prelude shook the wooden pew sending a sexual thrill through her. She ought to have a headache—but she does not. Shouldn't Phil quit and come to bed? In their apartment he gets tired before eleven. Oughtn't they to eat? Have the ducks flown away yet? Were the two of them going south for the winter but instead decided to stay here, in this aberrant, overheated city? She would go outside again to see, but she doesn't want to lose her chance to be lucky. If she misses her lucky pull, she'll never be a winner. So she stays and plays; she's allowed herself a week's salary in nickels, if need be. To win big one has to take big risks. The thin singer flashes her rhinestones, clutches her mike, and belts out, "I wanna know what love is…"

Finally Phil comes to find Lynn. He must have hit a losing streak, but she doesn't ask. They take the elevator up, leaning against the sides, eyes nearly closed. In their room they fall into bed. They don't even touch fingers they're so tired.

Even with the extra-heavy drapes on the window, knives of morning sunlight manage to slice through and pierce their sleep. They wake shielding their eyes. The thumping from below can be felt already; it seems to come up through the pipes, an urgent force from the red-carpeted, neon-lighted, all-night room. The casino calls to Lynn's mind an emergency room in a hospital, always open and ready. Casualties of love and war eagerly accepted.

While Phil showers, she hefts her little paper cup of nickels and estimates she has about four dollars' worth left. She's impatient; men take so long to shave. She glances through a throwaway she found on an ashtray in the hallway last night: *Las Vegas Bachelor Guide*: "Triple X-Rated Nude Dancers Direct To Your Room." "Free Limo Service To All Brothels." "The World-Famous Historic Chicken Ranch—The Best Little Whorehouse In The West."

She settles down in a chair to read:

> *What do a nutritionist and a classical pianist have in common? For one thing both women work at the Chicken Ranch and, like all the other ladies of the ranch, are accomplished, intelligent women with a*

*wide variety of interests. The women, who range from 18 to 37, have skills in such areas as nursing, teaching, real estate, farming, and finance. One of the ladies speaks five languages and is still studying. Though far away from their homes, they support the local Pahrump senior citizens' center, which indicates their caring support of their home away from home.*

Lynn thinks of how boring her job at the paper has become, how poorly it pays. What if she went out to the Chicken Ranch for an interview? There is a free flight, the paper says, from Vegas to Pahrump.

*The Chicken Ranch features a new eight-person jacuzzi offering private and group relaxation and enjoyment.*

She considers suggesting that perhaps Phil should take that free plane. Does she want him to have *that* much fun? She's been tired and unimaginative in bed for some time now, for at least as long as it took her friend to die. But she wants everyone to get as happy as possible. She wants to be genial toward the world these days, forgiving, generous. Everyone is struggling—who is she to judge anyone? Tears actually fill her eyes when she reads:

*The new wing at the Chicken Ranch is fully equipped to handle physically handicapped people with everything from the wheelchair ramp on the front porch to the specially designed lavatory facilities. Doors have been widened throughout for the comfort and pleasure of all visitors.*

The pictures in the pamphlet show girls in silk teddies, g-strings, and lace garter belts. All Lynn has in her suitcase is her Mickey Mouse sleepshirt since she thought she'd be sleeping at Phil's parents' house, possibly—if circumstances demanded it—alone in the guest room.

Phil comes out of the bathroom in a cloud of steam. With his hair wet, he's closer to bald than she's ever seen him. She goes to him and hugs him tightly, her few tears mixing with the drops of water still on his chest.

"I'm ready to go down," he says with a smile, letting go of her. "Maybe we'll have energy for a little hug later on."

"I hope so," she says.

He indicates a pile of red chips on the top of the TV. "I think I'm actually a little ahead," he announces.

"That's wonderful," she says. "I'm happy for you."


In a room as big as a gymnasium, the breakfast buffet (with the fifty-cents-off coupon from their fun books) costs only $2.50; for this they get herring in sour cream, bagels and lox, omelets, blueberry muffins, Danish, doughnuts, coffee. On the warming tray are chicken livers in gravy, chipped creamed beef, and blueberry blintzes. On another table is an array of fruits: grapefruit, watermelon, prunes, peaches, grapes, plums.

Lynn and Phil stuff themselves—they are both severely starved—while inspecting the hotel guests at the other tables. Everyone seems to be eating from at least two full plates. Everyone seems to weigh at least two hundred pounds. The women are dressed mainly in bright polyester floral pantsuits; the men tend to wear cowboy shirts and string ties. Each person has some piece of gold jewelry adorning his body somewhere.

Lynn wears no rings at all. Her only decoration is her digital watch with Clark Gable on its face. She doesn't glance at it; whatever day, whatever date it is, she doesn't want to know. She's caught up in the spirit of nowhereness, she deeply appreciates it.

"Should I call my mother?" Phil says.

"No," Lynn answers truthfully. "What for? Not now."

They decide to make a run for Lots o' Slots, which is right across the street. "Hang on," Phil says, and pulls her through the double glass doors into the oven of morning. She breathes through her mouth, hoping to cool the air before it sears her lungs. At the bus stop, a man is asleep on a bench, clutching a paper bag in his hand. Beside the bench is his wheelchair. Lynn sees he is lacking legs. But at that moment Phil yells, "Look!" and from above them a human form hurtles down a vertical chute from six or seven floors high into a pool of water.

"Would you go on that waterslide?" Lynn asks.

"Only if you'd go with me," Phil says. "Would you?"

"I'd go with you anywhere," she says. "I'd stick with you through thick and thin." She can imagine them paying the admission to Wet 'n Wild, climbing the circular ramp high into the heat of the sun and then taking their places at the top of the chute, hands entwined.

She wants to do it, shake him into action. But he's squinting, shading his eyes as he watches a second person shoot down the chute. He isn't capable of grand acts. She needs to remember that.

Lots o' Slots has a front open to the street; hot air occupies the first ten feet of the casino area.

"See you," Phil says, and disappears toward the blackjack tables.

Lynn takes out her cup of nickels and finds a circle of machines under a sign which reads "Progressive Jackpot." The jackpot increases one penny by each pull of the slot arm on any one of the machines. The present kitty holds $4,320.59. Lynn deposits three coins (the maximum for the highest win) in a machine, and it spits back thirty nickels on the first pull. Good, she pulls up a stool, though the heat is at her back. This machine is near the entrance, maybe it's really set to give back 97 percent, maybe it's "generous."

Beside her a young woman is seated, leaning her head against the glass screen of her machine. Her hair is tangled ash-blonde. She's wearing blue jeans and a pink-and-blue T-shirt. Her eyes are closed; without looking she regularly inserts three nickels in the slot and pulls the handle. She takes the nickels from the tin bowl at the level of her knees, drops them in, pulls; takes out more nickels, drops, pulls. She functions like a sleepwalker. There are four reels spinning on these machines: no cherries, no bells, no oranges, no dollar signs, no little smiling men—just black bars and white spaces, like jail uniforms.

Lynn hits again! Three out of four mixed bars show in a row and thirty more coins come down. Lynn's heart leaps up. The machine even plays a little tune, as at the start of a horse race, when this happens: "Dah-dah, dadadada, dah-dah!" Thirty coins are good for ten free pulls, ten more chances, using the casino's money, for the big jackpot.

The woman beside Lynn gets a double-long fanfare. Sixty coins tumble down. "Hey, not bad," Lynn says. She'd like to make a friend here. But the woman is busy pulling again, her eyes still closed. This time two sevens line up and two bars.

"That's *really* close!" Lynn says.

The woman half-opens her eyes. "Yeah, really," she answers, but she doesn't even glance at Lynn. She just keeps putting in nickels. Lynn wonders: if two sevens out of four line up, does that mean one is halfway to paradise?

The woman is searching in her handbag now, searching quite desperately. She dumps its contents in her lap—wallet, glasses, cigarettes, tissues—till she finds one last roll of nickels. She kisses the grimy blue-and-white wrapper. Then she takes off her wedding ring and hangs it on the call-button, which is there to call the change-girl for more coins. She smashes open the roll of nickels and starts pumping them in. She's crying. Her back is shaking and she's sobbing. For some reason, Lynn begins to cry, too. They both work hard for a long time with no music from the machine to encourage them. They go faster and faster. The laws of probability seem quite cruel, quite indifferent to their needs.

*Thunk, thunk, space, space.* Only two bars, not three, line up. *Space, thunk, thunk, thunk.* Three bars, but at the wrong end of the line. Playing here is like living. Nothing works out most of the time.

Lynn is almost out of coins. She has three three-nickel pulls left. Her buddy, who seems just about out, too, puts in one, two nickels, but hasn't a third. She scrapes the bottom of her handbag again, but there's nothing in there.

"It's all over," she states, looking upward, not to heaven, but to the jackpot sign, whose number had gone up by almost a dollar. Suddenly, like a snake, she slides off her stool and disappears out the door.

"Wait!" Lynn cries after her. Her wedding ring is still there, hanging on the button, a thin, plain little circle of gold. Lynn stands up to see if she can see her, to see if she's coming back. Maybe she went to get more money from someone, from her husband. But probably there is no husband. Lynn decides to put a paper cup over the slot handle to indicate the machine is taken; she will guard and protect it till the woman comes back.

But an hour later (Lynn has bought another twenty dollars' worth of nickels) the woman has not returned. A half-hour later Phil arrives at Lynn's back, ready to move on to some other casino.

"Look at this," Lynn says. She lifts the wedding ring from the button and holds it in front of Phil's face. "Someone went away and left this here."

He looks as if he doesn't recognize what it is.

"A wedding ring," she explains.

"Well, just leave it," he says.

"No, I want it," she says. "The woman isn't coming back."

"Then take it," Phil says. Behind them, a woman shrieks and jumps into the air. "Hey! A thousand dollars," Phil remarks. "That lady just won a thousand dollars, Lynn."

"Give me just one lucky nickel," Lynn asks. She puts the woman's wedding ring on her own ring finger. She is going to play the woman's last pull and will accept the result as an omen. If she wins the big jackpot with it, her life will change and she will be happy forever.

Phil hands her a nickel. She puts it in and pulls for dear life. But she doesn't watch. She walks out to the street with Phil and listens raptly for the tune, for the rhapsody, for the celestial music she dreams of. But all she hears is the tinny thunk-thunk of the thin winnings of other human beings.

The sun is setting over the desert when they leave Las Vegas for LA; they're blinded by the light. The clouds turn into sparklers, the sky ahead is an inferno, they can't go on. Just on their right, at the state line, is one last casino called Whiskey Pete's. The marquee announces:

# SEE BONNIE & CLYDE DEATH CAR
## 95 CENT BREAKFAST
## 10 oz. CHOICE NY STEAK $2.50

"Let's stop in the casino there," Phil says. "We can wait for the sun to set."

"Good," Lynn answers. "Maybe I'll be lucky."

Instead, within five minutes, she loses her purse. She puts it down between two slot machines and then wanders away with her cup of coins to some other machine. When she realizes it's gone, she gasps like a person who has won a jackpot. All the rows of blinking slot machines look alike: she's lost.

She dashes like a crazy woman up and down the aisles, confiding breathlessly to every passing cowboy and change-girl, "I lost my purse." She runs, she runs and looks in the dark crevices between the machines where she finds ashtrays, empty cocktail glasses, blackened paper cups, handy-wipe wrappers, and the curls of torn-open paper coin rolls.

"Oh, God!" She can't believe she's done something this stupid. Her purse, that puffy brown kangaroo-pouch full of her precious cards and keys and her silver whistle and her money and her can of mace: gone. *Where are you?* she thinks. *Why don't you call my name?* She sees Phil bent over his blackjack hand at a table with four other men who are bent over their hands. Luck, luck, everyone wants luck and she's sick of luck!

Is *she* lucky? She didn't die of AIDS, did she? She escaped seeing Phil's paralyzed father, she even has a wedding ring now she never had before. Is that luck?

Suddenly she nearly falls on her face over a platform displaying an ancient automobile she didn't notice on the way in.

The car is roped off and is riddled with bullet holes. A life-sized picture of Bonnie Parker in a long black dress is mounted on thick cardboard and is leaning against the front of the car. A companion photo shows Clyde Barrow, handsome and shrewd, holding a machine gun and sitting on the front bumper of what must be a Ford. For also on display is a letter addressed to Mr. Henry Ford, Detroit, Michigan, received there on April 13, 1934:

> *Dear Sir:—*
>
> *While I still have got breath in my lungs I will tell you what a dandy car you make. I have drove Fords exclusively when I could get away with one. For sustained speed and freedom from trouble the Ford has got ever other car skinned and even if my business hasen't been strickly legal it don't hurt eny-thing to tell you what a fine car you got in the V8—*
>
> *Yours truly*
> *Clyde Champion Barrow*

She studies the car in which the lovers were shot to death in an ambush in Gibsland, Louisiana, on May 23, 1934. *Now that's love* she thinks. *That's sticking together through thick and thin.*

Someone taps her on the back. She turns and finds Phil behind her, looking as handsome as Clyde Barrow and holding in his hand, awkwardly, as men hold purses, hers.

"Oh my God! Where did you find it?" She kisses him, jumping up and down, as he tells, happily, some garbled story about a woman who found it, brought it to the blackjack table where her husband was playing, how Phil claimed it as Lynn's....

It's only a purse. But she adores it and she adores Phil and she knows she has luck because she's just been rescued from a dark wood.

"Holy shit," Phil says, his arm around her, patting her shoulder. "Look at those bullet holes. Look at that smashed windshield. Will you look at that?"

"They really must have loved each other," Lynn says. Her purse, soft and padded, feels like a baby in her arms.

"That's what I call living hard and fast," Phil says enviously.

"That's what I call having fun till the very end," Lynn says.

"Like us," Phil says, giving her a hug. "You think maybe like us?"

# My Suicides

When I had been married for twenty-two years and had three children of my own, my brother-in-law tried to make me an accomplice to his suicide. My sister was hiding with her two sons in a battered women's shelter. Their #1 rule was "You may not call your batterer or abuser." Unable to reach my sister, he called me dozens of times a day, threatening to kill me and my family if I didn't tell him where my sister was, threatening to kill himself if I didn't get my sister to call him back within the next five minutes. Each time he called me, I turned on the tape recorder so I could later play his pleas to my sister, to keep her informed and partly to defend myself against being the only arbiter of his fate. When he called, he pled his arguments to *me*, made his bargains with *me*, declared his love for my sister to *me*, knowing that one way or another this information would get back to her.

When I was home alone I carried mace in my pocket. I hid the sharp knives in a hall cabinet out of his sight, but easy for me to reach in case I was forced to defend myself. I watched the street from behind my closed blinds in case he might be hiding in wait for me or my daughters. Twice he followed me in his car as I drove on my errands. He knew that sooner or later I would have to visit my sister, and then he would find her.

The police could not help me. They said a crime would have to be committed first before they could pick him up. A man sitting quietly in his car on a public street was not a criminal. When he called and begged me to invite him to dinner, I remembered the violence he had already done at his home, pounding his head through a wall in anger, biting his baby son on the scalp like an enraged animal. He had pulled a table to pieces, he had thrown a toilet seat at my sister because she wouldn't agree to sell the house so he could buy options on gold futures. When the price of gold went up and he blamed her for losing their fortune, he threatened her life, reasoning that death could not be worse than what they were already going through.

And I, in my quiet home, with my children and my good husband, in my measured and reasoned life, became an accomplice to his fury, to his grief—and I was filled with fear.

One Saturday night, while my husband and daughters and I were having dinner, he called and said if I didn't get my sister on the phone to him in the next ten minutes, he would be dead. This time, he said, he meant it. He knew just how to do it and he was going to do it. I begged him not to, that things would work out, that if only he would agree to have counseling, medication, he could come out of this—but just then my husband came up behind me and took the phone out of my hands. "Don't bother us anymore," he said. "Don't call here anymore. If you want to kill yourself, then just do it. But don't bother us." He hung up.

My children stared at him as if he had pulled the trigger himself. I began to shiver.

"How could you?" I asked my husband.

Still, I called my sister at the shelter and told her what her husband had said. She was sick then, with high fever. Her voice was as hoarse and deep as a man's. *I'll call him*, she said. *I'll tell him I love him. Because I do.*

Five minutes later she called me back to say no one had answered the phone at the house. She said she was too sick to care. She said she was going back to bed and cover her face with a blanket.

On Monday morning, I went shopping for food. No one had heard from my brother-in-law since the call on Saturday night. With my groceries in the car, I was driving across a street that went over a wash, a long corridor coming down from the mountains in which rainwater ran to the sea. In the wash I saw a family of peacocks. A peahen, dun-colored, drab, and her two chicks were walking slowly in the shallow rivulets of water and matted leaves. They seemed lost and confused. They walked first to one side of the wash, then the other. It was hard to imagine how they had got in there, or how they would get out. But my eyes were searching in vain for the peacock, the male with his bright colored fan of feathers, his shimmering energy, his beauty. But he was not there.

When I got home, I was carrying bags of food in from the car when the phone rang. My brother-in-law's sister told me that police had found him dead in his car, parked in a far corner of the top level of a parking garage, the hose of the vacuum cleaner attached to the exhaust pipe and coming in the rear window. He had been dead probably since Saturday. At the house police found his insurance policy flung on the floor just inside the door of the living room so my sister would find it there, his final message of fury and revenge.

My very earliest suicide was Tante Iphiga's daughter, Bertha. She killed herself on Easter Sunday when I was eleven years old. I was sitting on the front stoop of our house in

Brooklyn, watching the Christian families walk to church—especially the girls in their black patent-leather Mary Janes and ruffled dresses and big straw hats with ribbons streaming down the back. I envied girls who had been lucky enough to be born to a family that celebrated Easter. Jewish families had a few big holidays, but not one was as colorful and festive as this. In my mind I was humming Bing Crosby's rendition of "In Your Easter Bonnet..." when I was called inside the house and told that something serious had happened to our cousin Bertha—so serious that she was dead.

I remember trying to adopt a pained demeanor—I didn't know Bertha, and I wanted to stay outside and envy the pretty dresses of the girls in the Easter parade. (Bertha was the daughter of my grandmother's brother and his wife with the strange name of Tante Iphiga. All I knew about Bertha was that she had been dropped on her head as a baby, and was never quite right after that. She secretly married an Italian and continued to live at home till her mother found her wedding band in a box of her sanitary napkins. She went to live with the Italian who treated her badly. He didn't want children, so she began to raise pigeons on the roof of her apartment.

When I was grown up I learned what sketchy facts the family knew of her life: the Italian husband had a violent temper. He liked to go to big family weddings and funerals. Bertha liked to stay home with her pigeons. On her last Easter Sunday, he went off without her to a wedding. She stuffed towels under the doorframes and around the windows, put the cat outside, turned on the gas, and killed herself.

As a child I could see that this suicide caused everyone great distress. No one knew whether to feel sorry or angry, sympathetic or disgusted. They wondered if they could have been kinder to Bertha. She had a hard life. She wasn't pretty.

No one in the family ever visited her. I wished I had visited her and seen her pigeons. I was sorry she had married a cruel husband. And I was sorry she had ruined my Easter. What gave a person a good enough reason to want to die? I simply didn't know.

Another of my suicides was a woman my own age, a good friend, a well-known author of teenage novels, a woman who —as they always say of people who seem to have it all—"had everything to live for." She had a successful career, a devoted husband, and two beautiful children. Her record of publications and sales would be the envy of any writer. She lived in a fine apartment in New York City and she wrote a new book every year from October 1st to October 31st. Her rule for herself, which she confided to me, was this: "You must write ten pages a day or you will be shot." I admired her industry. She chose October in which to write her novel because it was a bleak month. Her children were in school, there was no sun in the sky, she wrote all morning every morning, and every afternoon went to a movie by herself. The books she wrote each October were her young adult novels; later in the year she would also write a novel for adults. Once a book was finished, there was the excitement of selling it, usually for a good deal of money. She was brave in treating subjects for young people: unmarried sex (a divorced parent having a love affair), a mixed-race romance, a boy who chooses to raise the baby his pregnant girlfriend wants to abort, and later in her career she wrote of euthanasia, the killing of an ailing grandparent by the heroine's father—out of mercy.

My friend's books were often removed from library shelves; she fought against censorship and traveled to speak out against it. We began writing to one another after our mutual agent died and we were both seeking a new agent. She gave me advice, personal and professional. She held back no secrets—she talked about money the way adults usually don't, telling me about the exact amount of her own earnings, about her husband's, about the advances she knew had been given to other writers. She spoke of secrets, of hers, her husband's and her children's. Without guilt, she read their diaries and letters. I was not so candid, I had a sense of boundaries she did not seem to have, which was also why I wrote with relative caution and she wrote so freely and bluntly. Once, when she came to visit me, I picked her up at the airport. On the way to my house, she began telling me the plot of a novel she planned to begin in October. As she talked with obvious excitement, we passed a burning house. Fire trucks were arriving, their sirens blasting. Smoke was pouring from the windows of the house, and people were gathered across the street to watch. My friend didn't even seem to notice the spectacle, her mind was somewhere else, her brain filled with the images of her book-to-be, her fantasies stronger than the burning reality at hand. During our visit, we talked for three days, stopping only to eat and sleep briefly. But mainly she talked and I listened. She was bursting with talk, her head was under enormous pressure from her visions and her ideas. Her daughters, like mine, were adolescent girls. We spoke about their new sexuality, how we dealt with it, what we feared from it. She told me she had taken her daughters to see a pornographic movie—that they might as well be exposed to such films in her presence as be shocked by them later, without her there to explain things. I was the one shocked—I was frightened that she wanted to control their minds to that extent, that she felt it was her duty to initiate them personally into aspects of life that were not her business.

When I visited her in New York, she gave me a blanket for my bed made out of the ties of her dead father who had been a psychoanalyst. She told me she was his angel of perfection—that she could do no wrong in his eyes. She confessed that after he died, she tried to kill herself, but had failed. She said it perkily, as if that had been just a mistake, over and done with. One wall of her library was filled with the books of Virginia Woolf who was her heroine and inspiration. She told me that any woman who came after Woolf and wrote a book was already defeated: Virginia Woolf had done the best that could ever be done. And died with stones in her pocket in the River Ouse at the age of fifty-nine.

We wrote letters to one another for fifteen years. Hers were single-spaced, four or more pages long, answered the minute she received mine, as I answered hers. What we had was a fevered long-distance conversation, two women typing madly at opposite ends of the country, consoling one another's literary disappointments, encouraging one another's ideas and plans.

In the library one day I read a devastating review of my friend's newest adult novel, a book about a woman who had been in a mental hospital for a year. I was astonished by the casual cruelty of the review, the way the reviewer had tossed out bombs of viciousness. A few days later, at lunchtime (I was frying kosher hot dogs in a pan, their grease was sizzling and spattering burning droplets on my hands) the phone rang and a woman whose voice I had never heard told me she was a friend of my friend and had some bad news for me.

"When did she kill herself?" I cried out. The woman, who was prepared only to tell me my friend had been sick and died (the newspapers said, a few days later, that her death was caused by "septic poisoning") had to concede that she had "taken something" and was on a respirator for ten days before she died. I berated myself. I should have known something was wrong because no letter had come for more than a week. Like all survivors of suicide, in the afterknowledge of the death, I knew I hadn't called early enough or soon enough...hadn't really cared enough or been alert enough.

"She was only fifty," the woman told me. Perhaps, like Virginia Woolf, my friend had chosen to escape her torment and bypass old age.

When I flew to New York for the funeral, I stayed with my friend's mother, a woman in her 80s who lived in a huge apartment near Central Park. The walls were filled with clippings of my friend's reviews, photos of her, framed awards, and snapshots of her two daughters. Together her old mother and I took a bus to the church where a gathering of writers and editors sang praises to my dead friend. Her husband told me afterward she had called him at work and told him she'd "done something." He asked her if she had taken pills (he admitted to me he had been hiding her pills for the last few months). He assured her he was calling paramedics and would be right home. He later learned from the paramedics that when they arrived at her door, she opened it and told them there must be some mistake, it wasn't her, look at her, she was just fine. So they left. Her husband was caught in traffic in Central Park. My friend actually went down to the lobby to get her mail (writers must always get their mail) before she collapsed. By the time her husband arrived home and called the paramedics a second time, she was comatose. Her family buried her at the edge of a river, with a stone on which was engraved "Beauty mysteriously unfolding."

My mother's sister, an old woman, didn't quite achieve her suicide but left enough bloody fingerprints on the phone, enough blood on the sink beside the double-edged razor blade, and pools of it in the bed and on the floor, to convince me it was a real act and not, as her psychiatrist told me later, just a "cry for help." In fact, my aunt called me a half hour after she slit both her wrists and the vein in the crook of one elbow to ask me where she should hide her diamond ring: "I don't want the crooks here to get it." When I first picked up the phone, her voice was low: "You have to believe me. I'm tired of living," she said. I replied, as I did every day, sympathetically, "I know. I understand how much you miss Uncle Moe, but there's nothing you can do about it. You have to wait and hope your feelings will improve." She said, "There *is* something I can do. I already did it."

"You did what?"

"I slit my wrists. Don't call anyone."

I stopped to think hard. I actually considered doing as she asked. I had watched my uncle die of lung cancer. I had seen the colored pen marks on his chest where the radiation was aimed, seen him unable to swallow because of his charred esophagus, seen the purple bleeding holes on his ankles, seen him gasping for breath under the oxygen mask in the hospital. I had also visited her a hundred times since her widowhood, sat with my aunt on her living room couch in the retirement home with the other old crones, smelled their smell as we all crowded into the small elevator to go down for the watered soup and canned peas for lunch. Why call for help and bring her back to that and the rest of it—her own decay, her inevitable stroke, her broken hip, her feeding tube (all of which I'd witnessed with my mother). These thoughts passed through my mind as I held the phone. Then I saw my husband walk by the doorway of my office and I blurted out: "It's my aunt, she's slit her wrists and doesn't want me to call paramedics."

"You have to," he said simply.

"Why do I have to? She doesn't want to live."

"You just have to," he said.

I got my sister on the phone and told her my aunt's wishes.

"You have to call paramedics," she said. "Or I will."

So I called the paramedics. My action was responsible for my aunt's ambulance ride, her ten-day lock-up in the mental ward of the hospital, the counseling with other crazies, a roommate who peed on the floor of their room at 2 am. During that period I had to go to her retirement home and clean up the blood, asking myself every second (as I threw away all her scissors, knives, pins, razor blades and screwdrivers) if I shouldn't have let her bleed to death and be done with it. Now we were all in for it—more old age, more grief, and death anyway.

We moved her to another retirement home and she went on living, had a stroke, lost her sight, lost her hearing and regretted every day that she hadn't done a better job with the razor blade.

On April Fool's Day last year, one of my students, a 23-year-old young man with a long blond ponytail, sealed his mouth with silver duct tape, put a plastic bag over his head, and managed to make himself die.

"The self has gone away and all the atoms are seething," he wrote in his suicide note, left on his website along with a photo of himself shown vaguely in shadow inside a screened window, his form already fading into the ether.

"Please don't cage it in a box and weigh it down with polished granite. Cremate it. And don't save the ashes in some silly container…toss them on the desert…I want to be a cactus next!"

His website offered a number of personal notes to his friends, many of his poems and paintings as well as the only story he had ever written (for my class) on the strength of which, he told me at our conference, he wanted to quit school and become a writer.

We sat that afternoon in my windowless office on the campus and discussed his future. He had read his story, titled "Generation X," to our class the week before. All my students were nervous about reading their stories aloud; sometimes their voices trembled or the pages in their hand shook.

My student's story was about drugs. Our class members were not surprised or even remotely disturbed by this: most of their own stories had to do with drugs and sex. His story involved a group of college friends who spend a few days hiking in the mountains and taking drugs. "Finally, the damn sun's gone. I'm trying to make my eyes as soft as I can… Little blue butterfly…carry me back to the clover fields of my childhood…taste it dissolve, the universe will soon be smooth again, no prickly dried blood clogging every pore. Why did you give us this shit, Timothy Leary?" In the last line of the story, my student wrote: "He rolls over and looks up into the valley: the distant mountains are bathed in early morning gold, a white veil of fog hanging before them: the promised land. Turning to Justin and pointing through the veil, he says, with a twinkle: 'Let's go there.'"

Where, exactly, my student's hero wanted to go did not seem ominous to me until the dean phoned me one morning and told me my student was dead. He had dropped out of school and had given away many of his belongings to his friends and told them he was moving to Santa Cruz to be-come a writer. He had told me—when he discussed quitting school—that he wasn't worried about making a living. He could work part time for his food. As for lodging, he still had keys to the lab and he could always sleep there. I had told him, as I felt I must, all the reasons he should not drop out of school: *you can't count on making a living as a writer, science is a more reliable field than literature. A life devoted to art is about as certain as the lottery.*

"I know all that, of course," he said to me, pulling his hand down the length of his ponytail. Had I been twenty again, I could have fallen in love with this young man, a gentle soul who wore his torment in his eyes, a physically beautiful boy— delicately graceful, blue-eyed, tall and slender. Of his farming family across the country, he said, "My parents don't know anything about me. They can't figure me out."

After our talk, he offered me his hand. His fingers were cold and damp. I wished him luck, I told him to be sure to stay in touch with me. A few days later, I passed a grassy knoll on campus and saw him stretched out, his hands behind his head, staring at the blue sky. He caught sight of me and sat up, guiltily. I smiled and nodded my appreciation, envying his youth, his poetic trance, his dreamy face turned to the sun. Not so long after, I had the phone call that told me he had killed himself and transformed his seething atoms into ashes for the cactus plants in the desert.

An informal memorial service was held for him on campus a month later. I and two of his other teachers spoke about him. A number of his friends were sprawled on the grass near the student center. His drawings and paintings had been taped to a nearby wall.

I told the students not to romanticize his death; I told them suicide was not a courageous act, and in his case was a waste. I said what I had to say—but I felt Hamlet's conundrum was at the podium with me. My student's friend stood and spoke about religion and Jesus, and how being born again helped him to understand the meaning of life and death and how he loved the lost young man more than ever now and knew he would see him again in the presence of God. I was sorry that someone else, another science student, didn't dispute or argue this in any way.

After the service, the registrar, who was my friend, came up and told me she was glad I took a tough line, not showing pity or admiration for this kind of death. We shared chips and guacamole dip with the others, and afterward looked at my student's paintings as if we were in an art gallery. One painting was of an enormous eagle with a beady eye who has, balanced on his rounded head, a tiny observatory. My student had clearly been making fun of man's puny attempt at "seeing" versus the deep black eye of the true seer.

Not so long ago I took a job on a suicide hotline after six weeks of training. Their office was in a double-locked room in an unused wing of a small local hospital. The room was tiny—one chair, a desk, a phone, a teapot, a few paperback novels. Someone had taped up a list of specific instructions to tell the callers: *Make yourself a peanut butter sandwich. Put on a sweater. Promise me you'll do what I'm telling you and call me back in fifteen minutes when you are calmer and tell me exactly where you live. We can help you. I swear you won't always feel this way.*

Each time the phone rang, I felt a shiver and the hairs on my arms stood up. "My husband knocked out my two teeth and won't let me get them fixed. He doesn't want me smiling at other men. He won't let me out of the house. I found his gun. I'm going to use it."

"Make yourself a peanut butter sandwich," I would say. "Tell me your address."

"I'm a sixty-year-old man with stomach cancer. I weigh 84 pounds. I'm in terrible pain and I have no family. I know a place where I can jump off the roof."

"Put on a sweater," I would say. "Pour yourself a glass of milk and promise you'll call me back and give me your address."

Usually they never called back. I scanned the newspapers the next day to see if anyone had jumped off a roof or shot herself. If I did get someone to confess his address, I would have the emergency team sent out. I wasn't allowed to ask the outcome of their rescue.

Often, in that little locked room, I got obscene phone calls. The same man called night after night. I began to welcome his calls, sensing the man's obvious enjoyment of life. "I'm picturing you without clothes. I'm doing it right now as I talk to you, honey. Unbutton your blouse for me."

"Do it all you want," I would say, "as long as you don't kill yourself. Call me back when you're done and I'll refer you to a place that can help you."

Some months after my brother-in-law's suicide, my husband, my sister, and I drove to a meeting of Survivors-Of-Suicide. We met in a shabby building in the city's downtown area and sat in a circle on torn vinyl chairs, eating packaged cookies and holding cups of tea. Each person was invited to tell his story—the parents of the teenage boy who hung himself, the daughter of the old man who, standing in the woods behind his house, shot himself in the mouth, the brother of the girl who put poison in her coffee and left a sign on the stairwell saying: "Beware if you enter. Danger! Cyanide inside."

The facilitator told us to try to see our guilt for what it was, helplessness in the face of an unimaginable mystery, and to absolve ourselves. "We who choose to live can never really understand why the person we love chose to die."

We all were urged to describe the thoughts that haunted us. We were called on, one by one. Haltingly, family members described a special memory: the knock of the police at the door, the endless ringing of a phone when the loved one should have picked it up, the baffling suicide note, the image of the locked car in the garage with a person slumped in the seat. My sister, who sat to my left, described the sight of the presents her husband had wrapped and arranged for her on the kitchen counter before he fled the house to kill himself. "He left us gifts," she said. "He left me a framed picture of the two of us on the beach. He left toys. He left a poster of Superman rolled up in a tube."

Those sitting in the circle nodded with understanding.

To my surprise, my husband, who sat to my right, began to speak.

"My three young daughters were in the room when their uncle called to threaten that he was going to kill himself. I saw the terror on their faces as they understood what he must be saying. I saw them watching the terror on their mother's face. I took the phone and told him to kill himself if he had to and stop bothering us."

My husband waited to be criticized. Everyone looked at him with compassion.

"I don't blame you," said the mother of a suicide. "They push us to the brink."

My sister took my hand. I, in turn, took my husband's. I could feel the kindly eyes of the survivors upon me. I shook my head. I could not volunteer the image that haunted me.

Privately, I saw my brother-in-law on my doorstep, begging to be let in as I hid in the hallway with mace in my pocket. I saw him alone in his cold and dark house without his family, frantically phoning me. But, since he had died, the picture that came to me most often was the sight of the puzzled peacocks: the peahen and her lost chicks in the high-walled wash that wove its way downhill under the city streets and under the homes of happy families and to the sea.

# Dogs Bark

THE PINK-ASSED DOG LADY whistles on her back deck to start
them off. Though I can't see her from my window, I imagine her sticking two fingers into her mouth, the way boys do
to make a shrill whistle, and her dogs begin their frenzied
response. She claps her hands to invite them to a higher
hysteria. I know dogs, I know how their jaws clip like scissors,
chewing air in an ecstasy of racket.

Her three dogs bark day and night. My husband and I have
a new arsenal of responses—we are better prepared after all
these years, re-armed after so many battles. In the windows of
the rooms down the hall are the Ultrasonic Scream and the
Electronic Guard Dog. The Scream, which may be set to "silent"
or "audible," is a high-pitched whistle that is guaranteed to
discourage the animals from barking and is set in motion by the
vibrations of their noise. The Guard Dog (originally designed
to foil burglars) will, at the rattle of a doorknob (or the racket
of a dog), burst forth with one full minute of fierce yapping.

We use these tools as required—the Electronic Guard Dog
is turned on when the greatest ruckus is required, as on a
Saturday morning when the woman's teenagers are asleep but
when her dogs wake us. This is when extreme pandemonium
is desirable—one explosive noise bursting upon another, each

setting off the volley which triggers the next: dog, *machine*, dog, *machine*. The Ultrasonic Scream is best used, on the audible setting, when the neighbors host a dinner party on their back deck.

I have become the crazy lady. I am the witch who haunts her own house, machines at every window, high-powered binoculars in the kitchen to spy upon the pink-assed woman's children as they go down the street. The boy, now sixteen, swaggers from their front door. Once he's out of sight of his mother's view (but still within mine), he lights the cigarette pulled from his pocket and tosses his match into the grass. We found his empty disposable cigarette lighter on our pool deck one day. He throws the evidence somewhere else, won't carry it into his own house. He's a handsome kid, already as tall as his father, the failed accountant who now drives a truck for the family business. But the boy is sinister-looking, too, a kind of rat-faced boy who never laughs, who swaggers, who advertises that trademark of young men, the one that sends the message: *I'm tough, I'm ready to fight, ready to fuck.*

He walks down the street to his buddy's house. His buddy's younger brother is the boy who feeds our cat when we go away, when we drive north to visit our daughter who lives in San Francisco.

The boy's sister is fifteen—just at the age when she is beginning to know her power. Also rat-faced—it's a family trait, the narrowed eyes, the cone-shaped face, the tight lips— she has the birthright of sex shining from her hips. We see her sauntering down the street, too—not with cigarettes but with her new round breasts shimmering under her V-necked T-shirt, with her low-rider blue jeans curving around her slender hips and splitting her crotch nearly in two with their tight seam. She runs her hand down the length of her blonde hair as she walks, as if caressing herself. She has a friend we often see with her, a mirror-image girl, the same slim hips, the same forceful crotch, the breasts. They never look toward my window—they know I am watching them.

I remember the day that the girl's mother, pregnant with her, wearing pink gingham maternity shorts, went around the neighborhood soliciting signatures from neighbors, asking them to state that the dogs were not a bother to anyone. Of course, *we* are the ones living six feet from their dogs. Every room we use, whether for sleep, talk, work, or love, is a broom's distance away from the bomb-burst of the animals' noise.

These children of the dog people own the world. There's a fortune waiting for them from their grandparents, the immigrants who came here to sell fresh flowers on streetcorners and now own ten stores that sell fake flowers and crap of every variety, from plastic Santa Clauses to Halloween monster masks and crude ceramic angels.

How did my husband and I become transformed into the horrid old farts, no better than the Russian woman who lived next door to my house in Brooklyn and threatened to throw scalding water on my head if I played ball against the wall on Saturday mornings? How did we, in our quiet lives, in our academic law-abiding personas, become The Nut Cakes?

We know how they see us, the pink-assed wife and her mustachioed husband; we're the flies in the rich soup of their lives, we're the people who exist to torment them.

"Get a life," Mustachio wrote us in a letter. "See a mental health counselor and stop focusing your hatred against us. Stop rustling the bushes to make our dogs throw themselves at the fence. Stop throwing stones at them. And stop sending cops to our house."

We, who never rustle bushes or throw stones, are peace lovers, yet we are at war. We read every day of bombs bursting in villages full of children, of grenades exploding in pizza parlors crowded with families. Rockets, missiles, tanks—desperate solutions to anger and pain, creating only fiercer anger and pain the same ways our dog machines create escalations in our war. *Kill me and I'll kill you back. When I kill you I feel better.*

We live in a city famous for its lack of crime. The Village of the Vines is the picturesque name for our town, which boasts the largest wisteria vine in the country. The police seem grateful when we call them about the dogs. They need crimes. Their crime log in the newspaper reads: "Bicycle missing," "Woman falls on streetcorner," "Unexplained noise in the backyard."

When I call, I pray the dog racket will continue till a cop shows up in his black and white car. Even if silence occurs (even if the dogs finally lie down and sleep), my husband and I stand at the front door and tell the officer about the disturbance and how many hours it's been going on. We tell him what quiet people we are, how we do nothing but read books and write them. We listen only to very soft music on the radio. My husband plays a clavichord—an instrument even *he* can hardly hear as he plays it.

The police in our city are impressively outfitted. Whichever cop arrives, he wears a thick black belt leaden with radio, a firearm, bullets, flashlight, mysterious leather snapped flaps.

"Please come with me," I tell the officer. "Look what happens when we go into our own yard." He will follow me around to the side of the house where the garbage cans stand. The instant our footsteps sound in the dirt, the biggest dog is snarling and bounding at the fence. His head comes over the top and he shows his teeth. His chops are dripping with saliva. The other two dogs join in. They all sound as if they are tearing flesh from bone.

The cop usually stands there without expression. (I am certain that at home he has three dogs just like these, and he loves how ferocious they are.) I recite to him some phrases from the city's lawbook, "Destroys the quiet enjoyment of our home to which we are entitled," "Breaking the noise laws," "No animal shall cause a sound that disturbs the peace and tranquillity of a neighborhood."

"You know anyone else who's bothered by the noise?" he asks. I point out that the closest neighbors are hundreds of feet away, others are blocks away. What he knows and I know is that in every house adjacent or behind or across the street live one or two dogs, beloved by their owners and whose noise is music to their ears.

Pink-Ass, as I call her privately, the mother of the rat-faced children, is a real estate agent. We've recently received a large number of postcards from realtors urging us to sell our house. "Low interest rates—the best time to move is NOW!" Evenings she teaches aerobic exercise at the Y. My friend who takes the class says my neighbor can't even jump in rhythm to the music. She's a blonde and her clothing is always pink— pink linen business suits, pink tights, pink sweatsuits, pink latex bicycle pants. Her shapely ass is packed into them— when I watch her from behind my drapes I can see the indentations of her soft buttocks under whatever she wears. Her flesh seems to have the texture of those foam beds the astronauts sleep on...of viscous memory foam, the kind you press and it remembers the shape of your fingers. What she and her husband do in bed is a place I try not to go to in my mind, but one thing I do know: whenever and however it occurs, I have never interrupted it, whereas they and their animals have been responsible for hundreds of occasions upon which my own love life has been blown to bits. My husband and I rarely attempt intimacy now. If we even turn toward one another in bed, we know too well what will interrupt and wilt us both.

In the early years, when the neighbors' first dogs were two Dobermans and a German shepherd, when the dogs' night-time volleys jolted us out of our embraces or out of a deep sleep, I'd wake, my heart pounding, and begin to catalog to my husband the reasons this existence was unbearable.

"Why tell me?" he would say. "Let's tell them." So at 3 AM we'd dress ourselves and leave our house, walk to their front door, and ring the bell. There we would wait, under the chilly moon, shivering, my own heart shuddering, till the truck driver would open his door and we'd say, "Your dogs woke us. Take them inside and keep them quiet."

"Sure," he'd answer above the racket, pulling tight the belt on his robe, "you just rang our doorbell. They're guard dogs. What do you expect?"

"Your dogs woke us," my husband would repeat calmly. "Take them inside. Keep them quiet," and we'd turn and walk back to our house.

Not that we had not said "please" at first, long before we came to their front door. No—we were extremely polite—and to be fair, so were they. We sent them little pleading notes, and they sent us big baskets of fake flowers with angels squatting in the plastic moss. But they didn't quiet the dogs.

"I LIKE to hear my dogs make noise. They're protecting us," Pink-Ass said to me one day when I saw her over the fence and pled for relief. "That's why I got them. I love to know they keep us safe. And you know something?" (She said my name for emphasis and mispronounced it.) "You know something? Dogs bark. That's what they do. Get used to it."

* * *

What will kill dogs? Onions will. Mushrooms and grapes in large amounts. Chocolate! As little as a pound will kill a small dog, two pounds a large dog. A mere four ounces of unsweetened baking chocolate can kill a big dog. And dogs love to drink antifreeze. One half teaspoon per pound will cause a dog's death in 12–36 hours. He will walk about with an uncoordinated gait while he is dying.

Friends have many suggestions. Put Ex-Lax in a hot dog and the dogs will shit all over their house. Enough Valium will keep them asleep all day. And rat poison is a sure hit: strychnine or arsenic.


At the first mediation, a strapping police officer invited us into his office and assumed the good will of all parties. Pink-Ass did not come, only her husband attended, and we set forth our case. My husband had a list of what was unacceptable to us and what must be changed. Mustachio stared at the ceiling and rolled his eyes around as we described our plight.

The cop suggested their building a dog run at the opposite end of their property, away from our house. He suggested simple training methods, a collar that emits a small shock, for example. Dog training. Building a solid fence where there was now a chain-link fence, to reduce the excitation of the dogs when we came into our own yard.

My husband volunteered at once to pay for half of such a fence. Mustachio looked at the police officer. "Hey," he said, appealing to the cop, "dogs are territorial. They're supposed to guard their property." Then he added, "If *they* weren't the kind of people they are, if they made friends with the dogs instead of throwing stones at them, the dogs would like them." Then he turned to us and said, "If you don't like it, sue us. You people like to sue."

*We people? We people who don't buy Christmas crap from your store to decorate our house? We people who don't even <u>do</u> Christmas? We Jewish people—is that what you mean?*

My husband put a restraining hand on my arm. I felt a kinship with my ancestors I had never experienced before. Later, when the meeting was over, my husband reassured me that the police officer knew exactly what was going on. "He knows the kind of guy he's dealing with." But I pointed out that as we left, Mustachio was still in there chatting with the cop, leaning over the officer's desk in a confidential manner, as if to confide to him what he didn't yet know: that we were cold-hearted, Jewish, animal-hating monsters.

Our cat is a Manx, tailless, tiger-striped, who walks silently on our roof at sunset, who licks my wrist every morning with his sandpaper tongue. A graceful pet, peaceful, self-absorbed, self-directed, focused on his own interests, never throwing himself against a fence, or caterwauling at midnight. His nature is admirable, his bearing aesthetic. He is the essence of beauty and grace. There is no comparison—our animal with theirs.

One night I am in a deep sleep when it seems an earthquake hits my chest. It is the harsh, guttural roar of the biggest of the dogs, sounding inches from where my head is on the pillow. The blast enters my deepest soul, enters the organs that maintain life, my heart, my lungs, and shakes them to the core. The eruption vibrates along my nerve fibers to the tips of my fingers. Dazed, I sit up, clutching for safety as when one is on

189

the edge of a dangerous dream, about to fall into the void. I find my husband's arm. It's 2 AM. In the distance, from the foot of the mountains, I hear the bestial cries of coyotes. A pack must have made a kill, they are all yipping and shrieking, a cacophony of violence which has set off the big dog. He roars. He wants to join the kill, taste blood.

I realize I am sick. Not just angry, not just distressed, but about to lose something essential, my sanity or my life. I put on the bedside lamp and in its glare I check my blood pressure on a battery-run device that I sometimes use. I feel the cuff inflate, stop, inflate again, stop, and inflate to the tightest position which suggests the highest possible reading. Before I see the numbers, I recognize the threat. My pressure reads something like 245/165—these are the numbers of potential stroke.

My husband leans over me. My teeth are chattering as I tell him what's wrong. He leaps into clothes and helps me pull on my pants, a shirt, socks and shoes. He drives me fifteen miles to the Emergency Room. A nurse takes my blood pressure, tells me to try to breathe deeply and slowly. We are made to wait another hour. A man who has just come in appears to be in the midst of an actual heart attack here, and a teenage boy has a broken bone bleeding through his shin. I am only in potential danger of dying, but they are at the brink.

We are there till seven in the morning.

Now I have pills to take, morning and evening. Four times a day I am required to take my blood pressure. Stress causes this sickness in me. Stress causes fury. Stress incites the oppressed to war. I picture the house of Pink-Ass and Mustachio going up in flames. I picture their children shooting heroin in the downtown alleys of the Village of the Vines.

* * *

We are interrupted as many as fifty times a day by outbursts of dog noise. I look for guidance on the internet. I find a product even noisier than the Ultrasonic Scream. It's called the Super Bark-Free:

*When a dog barks within 50 to 60 feet of this device it will respond by blasting the offending dog with a strong ultrasonic blast of 130 decibels. This blast can be effective for over 100 feet if placed in a line of sight to the dog and there is little or no foliage to buffer the sound waves. The level of sound is about the noise level as if a fire truck were to pass by you as you stood preparing to cross a street.*

I ask my husband if we should order this one. What's another hundred dollars or so? He is talking of suing our neighbors in small claims court, claiming loss of the use of our home, loss of income from work. I am a writer and how can I work? My husband is a historian, and how can he work? We read books about suing neighbors, we get the forms from the courthouse and fill them out but we don't turn them in.

*Do* we have a life or is this our life, this war? We mostly stay home. We like it best in our home, we haven't much interest in golf courses, synagogues, Las Vegas, or Broadway shows. We have grown daughters—we like to visit them, and have them visit us.

*Get a life*, Mustachio instructed us, *and direct your hate somewhere else.* Could it be we have no other life? Could it be we "get off" on this battle? My husband and I now seem to have lots to talk about, we are conspirators against an enemy. We whisper long into the night. Imagining solutions. Planning retributions.

The police officer in charge of city code violations rings our doorbell. She is holding an official piece of paper. "We've received a complaint that you put your garbage cans out at the curb several hours too early on the day before garbage pickup."

"We what?"

"Garbage cans cannot be put at the curb before 4 PM on Thursday for Friday morning pickup. We understand you put your cans out last week a little after noon."

"Who reported us?"

"I'm not at liberty to say."

My husband and I look at each other. "This is just a warning," the Code Officer tells us, and hands us the sheet of rules for garbage can appearances. "I won't cite you this time. You can check the city code on the internet for all the details. Just don't do it again."

When she leaves our house, my husband goes to his computer to look up the city code. Then he tells me to get on my sweater, we're going for a walk. We walk past our neighbors' house. What is he looking at? We have seen their house five thousand times. An ordinary house, much too close to our house—why did we not notice this when we bought our house so many years ago? Why did we not notice that although our house is on a corner, with a large backyard, and a spacious corner lawn, one side of it is cheek to cheek with *their* house? Could we not have foreseen these troubles?

My husband says to me: "Where do they park their cars every day?"

I reply, "In their driveway."

"And what does the city code say?"

"It says you can't put the garbage out before 4 PM."

"No. The city code says that every house in the Village of the Vines must have a carport or a two-car garage—parking for two cars must be off the street."

"*They* don't have a garage or carport," I say. "He parks his truck and she parks her car in their driveway and they've sealed up their garage to use as a room. In fact, I can see their son's Little League trophies sitting in the garage window."

"Exactly," says my husband. His lower lip moves up just a little. I know that look on his face. It means he has reached a moment of determination.

Pink-Ass takes to riding her bike at 6 AM every morning. As she leaves the house, she slams her front door with such force that our heads bounce from our pillows. Just as we fall back to sleep, perhaps a little before 7 AM, some kid picks up her son for school, and honks seven times for him to come out. *Da-dada-dada-da-da*!

Again the door slams. We are never permitted to wake naturally. We are forced from sleep into anger, our first emotion of every day.

An official letter arrives from the office of the District Attorney. Due to our many verified complaints, a formal mediation with our neighbors is now required, this time at the courthouse with an official DA mediator. The neighbors have also been sent a copy of this letter, we are told. The results of our calls to the police have created a potential criminal case— "disturbing the peace"—a bona fide misdemeanor. The letter informs us it is to our mutual benefit to solve the problem before it reaches the possibility of trial.

My husband and I appear at the courthouse at the appointed time. We pass through a metal detector, we enter a waiting room, and there, sitting alone, is Mustachio. He's really an exceptionally good-looking man, buff, wearing a blue-collared knit shirt that shows off his upper-arm muscles.

His mustache is dark, thick, neatly trimmed. He's younger than we are but not that young. His hair is graying.

Meeting him this way, without controls and not in a formal setting, is disconcerting. My husband nods and Mustachio says, "Hey, how're you doing?"

"Isn't your wife coming?" I have to ask him.

He shrugs and holds his palms up. Apparently not.

There's a map of the state of California on the wall and my husband turns to examine it. Mustachio walks over to stand at his side and also studies the roadways of California. I take a seat on a cold metal chair.

The men start to discuss the merits of state highway 5. "If I need to get somewhere in a hurry," Mustachio says, "the 5 is not so bad. It's fast. But the cattle ranch. Whew, what a stink when you pass it."

My husband agrees that it smells very bad. He says he prefers to take 101 when we go north to visit our daughter. You can see the ocean. I can't believe they're talking this way while we are waiting to kill one another.

The DA Mediator sits us down at a long table, he at the end, and we adversaries facing each other. He says, "I can sleep through anything, so I never understand these problems. But my wife, to her dog noise makes her nuts, it can send her climbing the walls."

He gets down to business, opens his folder, discusses how many times the police have been called out by us to the neighbors' house.

"Look," he says to my husband and me, "I don't know if you hear an occasional 'woof-woof,' or if this is really a problem. The only way you're going to get any further with this is if you buy a video recorder with a time and date stamp and record the dogs for the next six months or so. Then you'll have some evidence. It says here on the police reports that sometimes the officers hear the dogs and sometimes they get there and hear nothing."

I look at him. I thought he was going to mediate. I thought he was going to let us describe how our lives were falling apart. But he's actually all finished. "Tape for a year and then come back," he says.

We set the video recorder, which cost us $700, on the desk in my husband's office. We aim it toward the fence between our houses, and we crack open the window an inch. My husband thinks we should just turn it on and let it run day and night. I disagree. We would have to use thousands of tapes. "Only when we hear the dogs," I say. "Then we'll turn it on."

Our life becomes a sprint, across the house or down the hall or out of bed or up from the dinner table. When we hear the dogs, we turn it on. Our ears are cocked all the time. "Do you hear something? Is that them? No, it's stopped. No it's starting again! I'll go! You go! Turn it on. *Turn it on now!*"

One day I am in my husband's office and I hear a noise just outside the window. I see the face of Pink-Ass rise above the top of the fence. She's trying to balance on a ladder that's in her yard. She's aiming a little camera at our video recorder.

Astonished, I call to her: "What are you doing?"

"You should know!" she screams back. She uses my name but mispronounces it. She nearly falls off the ladder. "You'll find out soon enough!"

A letter arrives with the name of an attorney on it. He represents our neighbors. They are accusing us of filming their fifteen-year-old daughter as she gets undressed in her bedroom. They have proof of this. The lawyer is certain that any judge would deem this a serious crime. We must stop filming their house or they will bring a lawsuit against us.

As it happens, some small aspect of my former and almost forgotten life intervenes. A book I have written is published and I am invited to give a reading at the bookstore in the Valley of the Vines. My book is a novel, and its subject is the long and grueling death of my mother. I am surprised at how little I have thought about my mother in the months that we have been taping dog noise. We haven't stopped taping despite the lawyer's threat—we know we are not filming the breasts of Pink-Ass's daughter.

I dress up in nice clothes and put some color on my cheeks, a bit of lipstick on my lips. Many of my women friends are at the bookstore, sitting on folding chairs. I wonder that they are still my friends, they have heard nothing from me for years but the saga of the dogs. Copies of my novel are piled on a table, and I stand before a microphone and read a chapter of my book.

When I glance up at the audience, I see the friendly faces of my friends watching me. I think that maybe my life is not as awful as I have convinced myself it is. Here we are in a companionable environment, with shelves of books and racks of greeting cards behind the folding chairs. I am reading words that I wrote at some time when I was able to concentrate and they are heartening to me: I once had a mind that could work. I am a good writer.

When I have finished reading, my friends line up to have me autograph copies of my book for them. I see my husband's smiling face as he sits on his chair and watches me. I haven't seen him smile in so long. He's quite beautiful, such a handsome man, sitting there in his tan jacket, his hair quite silvery already. I love him so much, and I love all my friends, and I feel blessed, released somehow, from the tension that is always living in me.

Then I see Mustachio in the line. His eyes are downcast, but he's holding a copy of my book in his hand, and he's moving up toward me. My heart nearly stops beating. I continue to sign the book that's in front of me with a trembling hand.

My friend bends down and whispers, "What's the matter?"

"It's the dog neighbor, he's right here in the line."

"You're kidding," she whispers. She looks back and sees him. She knows the whole story. "Oh God," she says. "I don't believe this."

He's coming up to me. My husband is talking to some of my women friends and he is unaware. I don't know what to do!

"Hey!" Mustachio sets a book down in front of me. "I was here looking for a birthday card for my wife, and I happened to see you." He's lying, of course, this is not a man who comes to bookstores to buy birthday cards. He had to have seen my reading announced in the newspaper. "Sign it Happy Birthday to my wife, would you? Her birthday is tomorrow."

Wish Pink-Ass a happy birthday? Is he insane? She's out on the deck every day, whistling her whistle, clapping her hands, to incite her dogs to pandemonium, forcing me to run to turn on the video recorder. She knows that I have to dash through the house, run to turn it on. She's like my puppeteer, jerking my strings. Suddenly I understand why he wants my book: he will be able to prove that the dog noise has not hindered my work-output. If we sue him for loss of income, he can prove that I have been able to do my work!

He shoves the book toward me. "Sign it Happy Birthday," he commands me. And I succumb—I can't refuse him. I don't want to start an argument here. I can't refuse a paying patron my signature. I sign my book.

A week later, the phone rings and Mustachio says, "Hey, I read your book. It's not bad writing. You really write well when you're angry. But the kind of life you had with that bitch of a mother, I pity you. No wonder you're such a crank. Jesus."

"What do you think you are, a literary critic?" I cry, and hang up. I find myself shaking for the rest of the day. I don't dare measure my blood pressure. My secret life now sits in his house, in his hands. He knows my inner soul. I feel I have been raped.

In my files, I find a letter Pink-Ass wrote me at the beginning of our war, when her children were still small, when she sent us baskets of fake flowers. "Don't you know how important animals are in the lives of humans?" she wrote. "Don't you know how people bring animals to nursing homes to make the old people happy? Don't you know that animals are good for your health and can lower your blood pressure?"

I begin to think we should get a dog. A puppy.

One night when we are eating out, I drag my husband into a pet store. Puppies are playing on the shredded newspaper. They are yipping and showing their little pink tongues and needle-sharp teeth. They are beagles, they shimmer with life. When I was a child I had a beagle named Spotty. This is the only solution, I tell my husband. We get a dog and then we begin to love the yapping of dogs. We will become desensitized to what is torturing us. The puppy will become an extension of ourselves, and we will adore our dog and whatever sounds he makes. And then we won't mind our neighbors' dogs. We will understand. We will hold our puppy's trembling, throbbing warm body in our arms, and we will come to love all dogs. We will have something to love instead of to hate; we will be happy instead of sad. We will no longer be old farts, but we will join the race of mankind which loves dogs. We too will love man's best friend. I am ready right then and there to buy the littlest white and tan beagle. I'm already thinking of a name for him. Maybe Peanut Butter.

At the end of a year, we turn our videotapes into the police department. Ten six-hour tapes, sixty hours of nothing but continuous roaring, howling, moaning and yipping. Sixty hours of lunatic noise. The officer on duty gives us a receipt for the evidence and tells us it will be brought to the DA's office the next day.

"Hey!" Mustachio says to me when I pick up the phone one morning. "Do you know *there's a warrant out for my arrest?* Do you know that if I got stopped for running a red light *I could be thrown in jail?*"

"Really?" I say. "No, I didn't know that."

"You people," he says. "You people." And hangs up.

The doorbell rings the next day and a tall, elderly version of Mustachio is on my doorstep with a well-dressed older woman. They tell us they are Mustachio's parents. They are here to make peace, to try to fix things for their son. "I don't think he knows how serious this is," his mother says. "What can we do to have you people stop making these complaints?"

"It's very simple," my husband says. "Have him control the dogs."

"They're not really his dogs," she says. "They're hers. She won't even consider shock collars, she says they're cruel."

She looks with some interest into our house. She's sees my husband's virginal in the living room. "Oh, are you musical?" she asks. "We love music."

My husband invites them into our home. He gives them a tour! He's courteous and courtly, and shows them from our windows how close their son's house is to our living quarters. He allows them to inspect his clavichord, his harpsichord, he plays a few bars of Bach for them. I am resistant to this much openness. He even shows them where we sleep—"You can see how the dogs run just outside our windows," he explains. Maybe he feels they will have some influence on the dog people. I follow them around the house, saying nothing.

"It's been so nice to meet you," Mustachio's mother says as she makes her way back to the front door. "Music is such a wonderful thing." His father, the rich businessman, looks as puzzled as I feel by this intervention.

"Anything you can do to help will be appreciated," my husband says.

At dawn, we are wakened by a shocking blast of music. A boombox is on the neighbors' back deck, playing at top volume. I hear the words "fuck the cunt" and "shoot the motherfucker" and other lyrics about killing, raping, and dismembering.

"Hurry," I say to my husband, "turn on the video recorder."

"What for?" he says. He's baffled. We've already turned in our evidence. "Maybe it's just their kids having a party."

"At dawn?" I ask him. "Outside?"

My husband looks wan. I take a good look at him. This war has taken a serious toll on him, this loss of sleep, this constant conversation about who is winning, who will win, who will lose, who will die. He tries to convince me that this is just a game of wills, that in the greater picture, under the eye of eternity, this is nothing. A little noise from some animals. No real violence.

But he's begun to look at ads in the real estate section of the Sunday paper. He points out to me ads for condominiums that don't allow animals. He suggests we look at some houses we might buy.

"Move? I can't move. This is my home. I've lived nearly my whole life here. I love how you wallpapered the kitchen with the jungle wallpaper full of toucans. We had our babies in this house. It's filled with all our books, our pictures, the memories of every minute we lived here." I see that I could go on for an hour and get sentimental about all the meals I've cooked in our oven, all the underwear I've washed in the washing machine, all the tomatoes I've planted in the backyard, all the letters received in our mailbox, all the nights we've made love in our bed.

"Start driving around with realtors? With women like *her*! You know how much I would hate that. Move so the neighbors can win? So they can know they chased us out? Never!"

"Do you want to spend the rest of our lives talking about them and their dogs?" he asks me. "Do you?"

Do I? When one of our daughters comes to visit she asks me the same thing. "Mom, I think you ought to see someone about this. It's taking over your life."

When I try to tell her additional details of the battle, to recount the lyrics of the disgusting, obscene rap music that Pink-Ass is now playing at us daily, for hours, she says, "I don't want to talk about this, Mom. I've heard enough." Like Mustachio, my daughter thinks that I should see a mental health professional. She refuses to commiserate, she won't be a party to this indulgence, this prurience. With a shock, I realize it does have some of the aspects of a sexual fantasy—my guilty obsessing about imaginary encounters with Mustachio at which I argue my arguments with him. *Don't you see what you're doing to me? Don't you see how unfair it is? Don't you see how you and your wife have ruined my sex life? That even if I don't hear your dogs, I know that at any moment I will hear them. You live in my mind all the time, you and your pink-assed wife. You monsters!*

I drive to the beach on a cool and overcast weekday morning. I have been reading a book on anxiety control that suggests imagining a peaceful place whose details you can call forth with absolute clarity in order to reduce stress. Only our neighbors and their dogs come to me with absolute clarity. I hope that if I see the ocean I will be reminded of its majestic force and that its elemental powers will calm my soul.

Two men approach the surf wearing wet suits as I am busy taking photos of strangely formed swirls of seaweed. (My plan is to take home details of absolute clarity.) When I look up again, the two men are already riding their surfboards out to sea. One of them has a wire hook where his foot should have been. A shark has probably had a meal of that foot—and yet here is this powerful man paddling out to meet the next wave head-on. Would *he* have a mental breakdown from the barking of dogs? I can feel the thunder of the ocean almost under my feet, under the grains of sand into which I am sinking as I walk along. I seriously question my own character, my weakness, my willingness to be consumed by what in the end is just noise in an already noisy world.

When I get home, my precious, furry, pink-tongued Manx cat whom I adore is missing. He hasn't eaten. His bowl, on the back step, is still full. He doesn't return after dark. The chair in the yard where he suns himself is empty. While I was at the beach, my husband was in the library for most of the day to avoid the dog noise and says he hasn't heard anything unusual since he came home.

By morning, my cat has not returned. I sit by the window for hours. I see Mustachio's son swagger by on the street. He is with his buddy and the buddy's younger brother who used to feed my cat. I have to know something. I open the front door and call out, "Boys, my cat is missing. Have you seen him anywhere?" The three boys look at each other suddenly, trying to keep their smirky grins under control. I am hit with dread, a certainty that Mustachio's son has enlisted the younger boy—whom my cat knows and trusts—to kidnap him. The air leaves my lungs. I understand for a fact that my cat, who has lived peacefully with us for ten years, is dead.

Though I take a sleeping pill that night, and though I push wax earplugs into my ears, I'm wakened by a new noise. The clock says 4 AM. My husband hears it too—we both sit upright at the same time. "What could that be?" It's a burst of sound, followed by a chugging noise. It sounds like water is hitting the house, hitting the window over our heads.

"Let's go see." We drag out of bed. We put on our robes. We go into the front yard and see that a new, enormous sprinkler that has never been there before is now installed on the edge of the neighbor's lawn and is sending forth bursts of water against our bushes and our bedroom window.

"I can't believe they did this," I say. "Those bastards!"

Back in the house, we lie in bed holding hands and listen to the sprinkler till 5 AM.

In the morning I call the police. They connect me to the Code Officer who tells me there are no laws against sprinkler noise in the city code.

* * *

In the world, war is worsening every day. Bombs go off in the Middle East killing countless human beings. Synagogues are blown up by suicide bombers. We see photos in the paper of grieving mothers, bereaved wives, crying fathers. The bodies of children in coffins are photographed. Bombs are let loose, shrapnel slices the faces of people in the streets. Grenades take out whole families. Rockets bring down helicopters. The vulnerable flesh of people is torn to bits by declaration of government heads. At the same time, conjoined twin babies from a third world country are operated on by highly skilled American doctors, the surgery costing millions of dollars, to give them a chance at independent life. Technology in the interest of death. Technology in the interest of life.

A sprinkler—a simple thing, a simple technology. I feel as if it's killing me. My husband and I are forced to move to a room at the far end of the house where there is a hide-a-bed. We are now banned from our bedroom. Sometimes, trying to sleep in the narrow, hard, fold-out bed, I feel crushed and suffocated. If I am awake at 4 AM, I walk to my bedroom to check: yes, the sprinkler is on. It goes on every night. What words are there for our enemies? The language of their obscene rap music springs to mind. I begin to recite words for my own satisfaction. Such words come more easily to me now. *Those motherfuckers.*

My husband's hands are trembling. I notice it when he reads the morning paper. We now get calls from one young female district attorney after another. Our evidence is being passed from hand to hand. No one at the court wants to handle the dog case. No one wants to listen to sixty hours of howling and frenetic yipping. Each newcomer to the DA's office is assigned our case and somehow manages to pass it off to someone else. These young attorneys want murder, child abuse, crimes of passion. Each time one of them calls us, I want to tell her the whole, bitter story, every pressing detail, the history of every night that we have been waked, the story of every nap that has been destroyed. Of every hour of writing time that has been blasted to bits. Of every meal that won't go down our throats. How my daughters are beginning to see us as crazy. How our cat now lies at the bottom of some canyon, his dear flesh eaten by ravens and coyotes.

The neighbors have hired a lawyer who keeps delaying the preliminary hearing. Just when we think the evidence will be called forth, we are informed there will be a continuance. More time is needed. (More weeks ahead without relief from noise.) My husband assures me this is costing the neighbors a lot of money. That they are paying for every bark. I assure him money is not their worry—there is plenty more coming from the fake flower family.

We call the police to ask if the case can't somehow be expedited. The watch commander of the police department decides to give us a lecture. I know this boy, he used to be a page in the library, shelving returned books. Now he's high up in our police department. He says no one can ever win a neighbor dispute of this kind. Nothing will ever improve. He knows it, he has seen it dozens of times. Even he has a neighbor like ours. "The only thing to do is pretend they don't exist. Pretend they're dead. Don't acknowledge they are even living creatures. How much of your life do you want to waste on this?" he asks. "What percentage of your life is spent on this subject?" My husband, listening on the extension, says, "Probably 50%."

"So!" the officer says in triumph. "Half your lifetime. You're not young people, are you? How much more time are you willing to waste? Why don't you guys move somewhere else?"

"Where can we move where there are no dogs? Dogs will live next to us anywhere we go!" I cry. My husband and I have begun to despise all dogs and dog owners. When someone walking his dog waits in front of our house while his animal leaves a pile of shit on the lawn, I want to fling open the door and shout an obscenity. Why, I wonder, has the officer decided to philosophize with us about this matter? Does he want to buy our house?

"The nightmare will never end," he says. "It will only get worse."

Because I am a writer, the pen my only weapon, I write an editorial about dog noise.

*Cities take action about airport noise and pass laws about leaf blowers, but airplanes will pass over and the gardeners will move on: dog noise is ongoing, forceful, and unpredictable. City ordinances and enforcement are historically weak in this area. A dog's job of being "a watchdog" has largely been replaced by computerized alarm systems, and, in any case, how reliable is a yapping dog when anything will set it off and when a prowler can quiet it by tossing it a handful of biscuits? Noisy dogs, like car alarms, don't even raise a curious eyebrow these days. Those who work at home, or who sleep during the day, are most susceptible to disturbance. If we carried a set of drums into our backyard and banged on them at intervals during the day and night, we would be cited for disturbing the peace; yet the noise of dogs is as violent a disturbance as any uninvited sound and should not be regarded as a benign expression of animal life.*

The local paper prints it within days, and within a week the piece is reprinted in dozens of newspapers across the country. I begin to get e-mail from hundreds of desperate people who are going mad in their homes from the noise of dogs. My editorial is posted on a website named "nonoise.org." I have new friends. We sufferers have found one another in a hostile world.

A picture postcard arrives in the mail from our neighbors. It depicts three men, holding revolvers, aiming them at our faces. On the flip side it reads "Blah-blah-blah."

My husband, his jaw clenched, dials the Code Enforcement Officer and reports the neighbors' building violation. "Their house has no garage, no carport." He says to her, "I will withdraw my complaint if our neighbors will set their sprinkler to a more reasonable hour and control their dogs."

"I'm afraid these things can't be negotiated," says the Code Officer, the same woman who warned us that our garbage cans were put at the curb too early. "They will now be cited. They will have to rebuild a functioning garage. But you know" she adds, "it will cost them a lot of money. They'll be very angry."

Mustachio's mother phones me. "What's wrong with you people? No one has ever caused my son so much trouble as you have. We have had eleven dogs in our lifetime, and no one has ever complained."

"Perhaps you control your dogs," I say. "Perhaps you are less selfish than your son and his wife." I am sorry we ever let this woman step inside our home.

"Of course," she says. "We always take our dogs in at night. But how does my son's garage hurt you? Do you go up and down the streets, reporting everyone's garage?"

"Your son's dogs have hurt me," I tell her, though why I am confiding in her I can't be sure. "My blood pressure is dangerously high."

"Well," she says, "everyone has something. My son's wife has a life-threatening illness. She has to go to meetings about it."

"She looks very healthy to me," I say. "The picture of health."

"You have no idea what problems my son has," she says.

The neighbors go away on vacation. I see his truck leave, piled with bicycles and surf boards. They take their dogs with them and their daughter, but leave their teen-aged son at home. The rat-faced young man brings his friends to the deck at the back of the house every night. I go into my backyard and listen at the fence. I can see candlelight flickering on the wall of their house. I smell the smell of marijuana being smoked and hear young men's smarmy low voices laughing.

I tell my husband to come out and smell the smoke.

"We could have them busted," he says. "Call the police."

"These kids are dangerous. They killed my cat. They could do something to us."

"I'm ready for that. I'm waiting for that," he says.

I picture a car driving by our house with automatic weapons pointed at our kitchen window. I see us both lying dead in a pool of blood.

"I don't want to be in this war anymore. God, I hate this war."

"No one wants to be in a war," my husband says, "but when there is one, you have to fight."

Still, we don't report the boys smoking pot. It's irrelevant to our cause.

A trial date is finally set. The young female DA lets us know our neighbors feel they have done nothing wrong and they're "taking it all the way." Though she offered them a deal to muzzle the dogs for six months, they refused. She says a jury will have to be chosen. We will be called as witnesses. We need to prepare our story. "This is very expensive for the state," the DA tells us. "No one is happy about this trial. Decent people usually make accommodations before a dog case gets this far. In fact, we've never had a trial in this courthouse about dogs before."

Is she saying we're not decent people? Or is it the neighbors? She sits in our living room in a fashionable suit, a very short skirt and mid-calf leather boots. She's under thirty, and she jangles her earrings impatiently. The DA warns us that our neighbors have conscripted other neighbors all around the block and even on the next block to testify that the dogs in question make no more noise than any other dogs. At least two of the neighbors are going to testify that we complained about their animals: a noisy parrot and noisy dogs, although this occurred twenty years ago. "They want you to seem like nut cases. They say you want to control everyone."

"But will we get a chance to tell our story?"

"Probably not. We may not even be given a chance to play any of your tapes. The judge doesn't have time to listen to barking. But I can question you as to what's on them. Just be dressed and ready to go on the day of trial. I'll call you as soon as I know the time you should be in the courtroom. And tell the truth." It's clear she isn't going to coach us or counsel us. She's out the door.

\* \* \*

My wardrobe is seriously lacking. My husband hasn't worn a tie since his father's funeral. We rehearse with each other— what to say, what not to say. "Don't say too much," my husband warns me. "You always say too much." I am shocked to think he has held this opinion of me and never told me this before.

"How can they select a fair jury?" I want to know. "Dogs are man's best friend."

"Maybe they'll find some people like us. Who haven't slept a full night in years."

Pink-Ass has taken to riding her bike up and down the street. She passes the front of our house where we sit in our kitchen having breakfast. On cloudy mornings, when the kitchen light is on, we can be seen as brightly lit as if we were on a stage. She wears a sinister-looking pointed bike helmet, and she rides back and forth, peering into our window as she rides past.

"What's this about?" I ask my husband. "Let's shut the blinds."

"No. That's what she wants us to do. To make a response."

Her little rat face peers at us each time she pedals by, her eyes narrowed with anger, her soft pink ass bouncing slightly on the hard seat of the bike. She passes by a dozen times while our coffee and toast go cold.

"Ignore her," my husband says. "It's called intimidation. We will not be intimidated."

I dress myself on the day of the trial. I think of the psychology behind my clothes. Rape victims are always told to dress demurely. Murderers usually have on a suit and tie.

Of what am I a victim? How will I present myself? How will I defend myself? I have to remember it's the state bringing the criminal case against the neighbors—we are only witnesses. The police records document the crimes. I simply have to tell the truth.

We wait all day for the DA to phone us. My stomach is heaving. My husband plays the piano all afternoon, he plays something loud and obnoxious. I am disgusted by every one and every thing. I don't see the point of living.

At 4:45 PM, I call the courthouse. Our DA has gone home for the day. There is no information about our trial. The receptionist can't connect me to anyone. The offices are empty. Try tomorrow.

"They took a plea at the last minute," our DA tells us when I finally reach her the next day. "The judge advised their lawyer that she didn't want to bother with this case and if they knew what was in their best interest, they'd not insist on a trial."

"Therefore?"

"Therefore they pled 'nolo contendere' and the judge dismissed five of the six criminal charges, reduced that one to an infraction, and fined them $100."

"Which means?"

"Which means that it's all over."

"But what did the judge tell them about the *dogs*! Did she tell them to keep them quiet?"

"The judge asked for no sanctions," our DA tells me. "I'm really sorry about that. I wish you luck on that."

"The law is a motherfucker," I tell my husband. "The judge is a motherfucker. Our DA is a motherfucker."

"Calm down," my husband says. "Don't be that way."

"It's over?" I scream at him. "After all those years, all that taping, and calling police, and begging and crying and going to the ER and keeping notes, it's now over? They were fined a hundred bucks and that's IT?"

"They essentially pled guilty. But don't worry, we're not done," my husband says. His tone is ominous.

But I feel I am done. Done in. Dead. I burrow into bed like a creature in its cave. I must have dark and quiet. Under the quilt I scream out loud. "Motherfuckers, fuck you all!"

That night, I follow my husband as he takes some of our leftover chicken out to the side of the house. When he rattles the garbage can, the head of the biggest dog comes flying over the top of the fence, his jaws slathered with drool, his voice like thunder. My husband offers the chicken to the dog on a plastic fork. The dog devours it, pulls it so fast out of my husband's hand that the fork goes into his mouth with the meat. The smaller dogs take scraps through the fence, also.

"And this isn't the only way," he says. "We have other options. This is just the beginning. I'm not going to let you suffer anymore. Just be patient. Little by little, we'll make progress. The right time will come. Save all our scraps from now on."

I want to try to recover my sanity. I remember that I used to write books and that in order to be human, I have to find a way to do my work. I can't work at home. I feel an aversion to every room of my house, as if horrors and atrocities have happened in them. They are not habitable.

"I'm going out," I tell my husband. I have my laptop computer in a little carry-case and my purse over my shoulder.

"Where are you going?"

"I don't know, but I can't stay here. Don't ask me anything else. I don't want to talk to you." It's not fair, I know, to be angry at him. But he's a man. He should have done something. He should have silenced the neighbors' dogs for me. He should have protected me. What good is he? He knows how I feel about this. He knows I think he has failed me.

"Please," he says. "I love you. We're not done yet. It isn't over yet. I told you that."

"It's all talk," I say. "All talk and no action."

I drive to McDonald's. I buy coffee and take my laptop to a back table and sit down. Some workmen are eating Big Macs and some teenage girls are drinking shakes. I am not at home and nothing can bother me here. I hear laughter. I hear fries sizzling in hot oil. I hear workers yelling, "Two Filets-O-Fish and Chicken Nuggets with Barbecue Sauce." This is noise that can't touch me. My excellent hearing is not a liability here. I am safe. I am going to live here forever. I can sleep in this booth. I can eat all my meals here. Why would I ever go home?

I begin to write my story. Some story, maybe the story of the dogs. I am deeply engaged in my thoughts, flowing along with them, lost in them, so utterly grateful they are arriving in my mind that I am almost ecstatic.

"Hey, mind if I join you?"

When I look up, Mustachio is sliding into the seat opposite mine with his tray.

"Do you mind if I talk to you?" he asks. "Is that okay?"

"I don't know," I say. He looks so familiar to me, almost like an old friend.

"We're losing our den because of you," he says.

"We're losing our bedroom because of you," I reply.

"You guys aren't really so bad. I know that."

"No, we aren't bad."

"The dogs do make a fucking racket."

"Yes, they do."

"All these years wasted."

"Look, what are you getting at? I don't understand this."

"I'm having migraines," he says. "And I'm sick of it. My kids don't even want to walk past your house. They're afraid of you."

"Yes, I'm sure your kids are very sensitive."

"I'll tell you something. I can take or leave the dogs. They're hers. When they die, that's it. No more dogs. But you know, the big one? The one you hate? He's really a pussycat."

"If you're going to defend that animal, then please leave. I have work to do."

"You really are a pretty good writer."

"I don't want to discuss that either."

"Are you and your husband planning to take us to court again? A civil case?"

"We're thinking about it." Could it be he's afraid of us? This is the conversation I've been having with him in my mind for years. Is it possible I have been in his thoughts as many hours as he's occupied mine?

"Maybe we could make a deal."

"I don't imagine your wife would want to," I say.

"She's not well."

"She looks so healthy."

"Yeah, she does look healthy. She's the picture of good health."

"Pink cheeks," I say.

"Yeah, she's very pink."

"She plays that disgusting rap music at us every day."

"I told her to cool it. She's losing interest, I think."

"Installing that noisy sprinkler was a vicious act."

"Well, you had it coming. But hell, I might reset it—how about six in the evening? Would that work?"

"My cat disappeared right after you learned there was going to be a court case."

"Hey," he says. "You think I would hurt an animal? You and I must have this mutual paranoia...I think *you* guys might hurt *our* animals."

"It hasn't happened, has it?"

"You have no clue how much money you've cost us," he says.

"You have no clue how much grief you've caused us."

He stops talking and starts eating his Big Mac, drinking his Coke. "All those years. We could've had you over for barbecues."

"Lost opportunities," I agree. "Your wife and I really wouldn't get along."

"This is bizarre," he says, "talking to you like a human being."

"But what's going to happen now? When we both go back to our houses? Same as usual?"

"It depends. I could get the dogs muzzles. You think I like that racket? I'd have to convince my wife. She likes all that barking. She loves it."

"Your wife is...very athletic."

"Yeah, isn't she? She rides that exercycle like there's no tomorrow. Where does she think she's going?" He finishes his Coke. "What a waste," he says. "What a shitty fifteen years or so. It's too bad."

"It is too bad," I agree.

He motions to my laptop. "I'm sorry you couldn't get your work done. You're really pretty good."

"Don't worry about it. I'll get back to it."

"I've got to go now," he says. "This is our busy season. I've got to pick up some holiday junk."

"Junk? You light up your house with that Christmas stuff every year."

"Yeah, a fringe benefit. Free reindeer. Free fucking Santas. As many holly wreaths as I can stick up my ass." He stands up. "So I'll see you over the fence or something."

"I'm sure you will."

"Just don't sue us, okay?" He takes his tray with him and dumps the leavings into the trash bin. He turns once and waves at me. Through the window I watch him get into his truck, the truck I have seen parked in his driveway every day for years. I am so elated, so wild with emotion. Is the war finally over? Can we finally live now?

On the way home, I stop at the Chinese market and buy ten pieces of lucky bamboo. I am going to put the plants in small glass vases all over the house—I've always wanted to have some of these beautiful little trees. Now I feel luck is possible, luck is about to grace our lives.

"This nightmare may be over," I tell my husband when I get home. He is sitting in the recliner in the living room, staring at a painting of a peacock we hung on the wall thirty years ago. "We may get some peace," I continue, telling him some of the details of my meeting with our neighbor. I tell my husband our neighbor is afraid we might take him back to court, he's willing to call some kind of truce. He's going to reset the sprinkler, he's going to control the dogs, let us get on with things. "I don't know if it will really happen, but he seemed sincere."

"I did it," my husband says.

"You did what?"

"I did what you wanted me to."

"What! Exactly what are you telling me?"

"You don't need to know the details," he says. "It's better if you don't."

"Oh my God," I cry. "*Oh my God.*"

"I told you it wasn't over yet. But now it is."

In the morning, two cops are on our doorstep. I know them both, they have both been here many times to take complaints about the dogs.

"Do you mind answering a few questions?" one officer asks us. We invite them in. They tell us what the problem is. We tell them we know nothing. They want to know if we're sure about that. After all, we've had a long-standing neighbor-dispute. We might know something. We might have something to tell them. We say we're sorry, but we know nothing about any of this. Nothing at all.

That night, sleeping on the fold-out bed, I automatically wake up at 4 AM and make my way through the house to our real bedroom. I listen. Of course, the sprinkler is banging away. I spend the rest of the night there, alone in our old bed. I listen to the swish-chug-chug of the Rainbird hitting the window over my head. At dawn the door slams. Then later, there is the honking of the horn and the door slams again. But there is no barking.

With the passage of days, my fear lessens. There is no longer rap music playing from the deck. There is a void, a vacuum from the house of the neighbors. I wonder if we can stand this much silence. My husband and I have very little to say to each other.

It's as if a long drama has ended. The play is over, the curtain has come down, and the two of us sit in the audience, unable to stir from our seats. I feel tearful much of the time. My husband has taken to playing the piano as loudly as possible. He has abandoned his virginal, his clavichord, his harpsichord. He plays my mother's old piano as if he is chopping wood.

I sit in the backyard and read books. I often think about dogs. I think that it wasn't even their fault. I look at photos of my beagle named Spotty and remember how much I loved him. I leaf through an old copy of "The Hound of the Baskervilles" by Sir Arthur Conan Doyle and read:

*A hound it was, an enormous coal-black hound, but not such a hound as mortal eyes have ever seen. Fire burst from its open mouth, its eyes glowed with a smouldering glare, its muzzle and hackles and dewlap were outlined in flickering flame. Never in the delirious dream of a disordered brain could anything more savage, more appalling, more hellish be conceived than that dark form and savage face which broke upon us out of the wall of fog.*

I begin to write again. I am writing something about dogs. Two months have passed and the police have not been back. I believe we are safe. My husband and I decide to buy a real bed for the room where we now sleep on the hide-a-bed. We will make the den our permanent bedroom. We have lost a room, but so have our neighbors. We have seen workmen there, installing a garage door in what was formerly their kid's trophy room.

I am at my desk one morning, deep in my thoughts, when I hear a tremendous blast. I drop my pen. The house is actually vibrating from the noise. Before it comes again, a thunderous and deep howl, I know what it has to be.

A new dog is barking.

"No," I say aloud. "No, please."

But once I get outside to the fence I see it's true. An enormous dog is there—as big as a horse. The smell of shit blows toward me in the wind. A new pet is there for Pink-Ass, a new protector. Her husband has cancelled our agreement, he has failed to protect me.

A bear of an animal is standing on the other side of the chain-link fence. He's a mastiff, with a great wrinkled jaw and black eyes. The instant he sees me he barks with the sound of a primal roar. His entire body shudders as he barks— shoulders, haunches, jowls. He barks and barks till I run into the house, my hand on my chest. My husband comes toward me, his eyes shocked. My heart is palpitating so hard it will surely fly through my chest wall. The truth comes over me like a pall. It is what Mustachio's wife told me long ago—the absolute non-negotiable truth that has till now escaped my understanding. Dogs bark.